**"I am absolutely not going into those woods, especially if there are killers on the loose," Kayla said.**

"Hey, Joe," a gruff male voice yelled. "There's a car in the ditch."

Two men stepped out of the forest about fifty yards away. Heath grasped her hand and pulled her into the shelter of the woods. As they watched, the men crossed the road to her vehicle and the younger one climbed inside and looked around. The trunk popped open and the older man reached inside and opened one of her suitcases.

"They can't do that." She took a step, but Heath halted her, a finger to his lips.

The men looked in their direction, the older one lifting his rifle. A shot rang out and a bullet hit the boulder where they had stood moments before.

Heath turned and ran, pulling her with him, deeper into the woods. Her heart pounding in her chest, Kayla ran as fast as she could, following Heath's movements, the gunmen close behind. So much for her declaration that she wouldn't go into the woods. Now she simply had to figure out how to get out of them, alive.

**Rhonda Starnes** is a retired middle school language arts teacher who dreamed of being a published author from the time she was in seventh grade and wrote her first short story. She lives in North Alabama with her husband, whom she lovingly refers to as Mountain Man. They enjoy traveling and spending time with their children and grandchildren. Rhonda writes heart-and-soul suspense with rugged heroes and feisty heroines.

### Books by Rhonda Starnes

### Love Inspired Suspense

*Rocky Mountain Revenge*
*Perilous Wilderness Escape*
*Tracked Through the Mountains*
*Abducted at Christmas*
*Uncovering Colorado Secrets*
*Cold Case Mountain Murder*
*Smoky Mountain Escape*

Visit the Author Profile page at LoveInspired.com.

# SMOKY MOUNTAIN ESCAPE

## RHONDA STARNES

**LOVE INSPIRED SUSPENSE**
INSPIRATIONAL ROMANCE

 **LOVE INSPIRED® SUSPENSE**
INSPIRATIONAL ROMANCE

Recycling programs
for this product may
not exist in your area.

ISBN-13: 978-1-335-63873-1

Smoky Mountain Escape

Love Inspired
22 Adelaide St. West, 41st Floor
Toronto, Ontario M5H 4E3, Canada
www.LoveInspired.com

**Printed in U.S.A.**

# ONE

Sheriff Heath Dalton wiped the rain out of his eyes, tilted his head and pulled his poncho hood lower, attempting to encourage the rain to run off his hood instead of into his eyes. "You better appreciate what I'm going through for you, little brother," he muttered under his breath.

His only vacation since he'd taken the office of sheriff two and a half years ago, and Heath had allowed Parker to convince him to go on a solo camping trip and test gear for the adventure camping supply store Parker had opened in Barton Creek, after he'd received an honorable discharge from the marines following a career-ending injury. Oh, well, at least Heath could testify that the hammock flap had done its job and kept him dry overnight. It had also been nice to sleep hanging between two trees as opposed to being on the wet ground. Other than that, the negatives were currently outweighing the positives.

The last three of his five nights on the trail had

been soggy. He had been planning on a leisurely hike back to his truck and had really hoped the rain would have moved out of the region by now. But the plan to sleep in and enjoy a hot breakfast over a campfire had dissipated when the latest storm had rumbled past a couple of hours before daybreak. Of course, none of that really mattered. Heath was glad his brother had moved back to the area and would do whatever he could to help support him and ensure his camping supply business was a success.

He glanced at the sky. Dark gray clouds hung low on the horizon. It looked like the rain event wouldn't end soon. The meteorologist had really missed the prediction for the week. When Heath had checked the weather forecast prior to his hiking trip, there had only been mention of scattered showers in the forecast. The chance of even that slight amount of rain had been less than twenty percent. But that had been six days ago. And weather was unpredictable, especially in late April in East Tennessee. Thankfully, the thunder and lightning had only lasted a couple of hours overnight and the weather had not gotten as severe as it could have this time of year. When the storm had awakened him, he'd lain in the hammock listening for the telltale train sound of a tornado. Unable to go back to sleep, he'd waited until the storm system had passed, leaving behind a steady drizzle, packed up and hit the trail,

The Lord is my shepherd; I shall not want.
He maketh me to lie down in green pastures:
he leadeth me beside the still waters.
He restoreth my soul: he leadeth me
in the paths of righteousness for his name's sake.
—*Psalm* 23:1–3

In loving memory of my mom, whose happy place was the overlook at Newfound Gap inside the Great Smoky Mountains National Park. It's been fifteen years, and I still miss you! Love you forever!

more than ready to get home, take a hot shower and get into dry clothes.

He prayed the days of rain hadn't caused flooding, making the bridge impassable. If it had, he might be stuck sleeping in his truck tonight. The day Heath had started his hike, he'd parked his truck at the ranger station by the end of the trail closest to Barton Creek. Then his good buddy, Sean Quinn, a retired Atlanta PD detective, had driven him to the Elkmont Campground inside the Great Smoky Mountains National Park and dropped him off, giving him seventy miles to hike. Thankfully, he had planned for his last day of hiking to be his shortest. By his estimation, he'd already covered three of the seven miles between him and the end of the trail. He should make it to his vehicle by early afternoon and hopefully navigate his way out of the remote area on the curvy two-lane road that led back to Barton Creek well before sundown.

Heath glanced at his watch: 9:15 a.m. Time to pick up the pace.

He followed the trail, hugging the side of the mountain to block as much rain as he could. After the drought they had experienced the past four months, Heath knew he should be thankful for the much-needed precipitation. He just wished it had held off a few days. If the waters in Barton Creek had risen as much as he feared, his deputies were likely working overtime to keep the citizens safe.

Two hours later, he paused and shifted the weight of his pack. Barring any unforeseen circumstances, he should make it to his vehicle in three and a half hours. If it wasn't for having to walk in the rain, against the wind, he could cut that time by half. He rolled his shoulders.

"Can't you shovel any faster? At this pace, it'll be midnight before we get home." An annoyed male's voice broke through the morning silence.

"Yeah? Well, if we had dumped his body in Fontana Lake, like I'd wanted, we would be at home right now."

*Body.* Heath stiffened, every fiber in his being at attention. He looked around. Where were the men? With the wind and rain, it was difficult to tell if they were nearby or far away.

"But no-o-o..." Anger thundered from the second unknown male. "You insisted we hike into the wilderness and bury him. In the middle of a downpour, no less. So, you dig the grave."

Heath had to find the men before they slipped away. He patted his chest, feeling his Glock tucked snuggly into the inside pocket of the lightweight jacket he wore under his backpack. The material of the poncho keeping him and his pack dry rustled. He jerked it over his head and wadded it up. Ignoring the drizzling rain that quickly soaked through his clothing, he shrugged out of his backpack, shoved the poncho into the front pocket and tossed the pack between a copse of shrubs and the mountain wall.

The mystery men were in a heated discussion. Bits and pieces of their conversation floated to him. Heath needed backup. He pulled out his cell phone. No service. Tamping down his frustration, he silenced the phone—in case he received one of those annoying telemarketing calls if he stepped into an area with service—and shoved it into his pocket. He'd have to deal with the issue at hand and then worry about getting a crime team out here.

Following the sounds of the arguing men, Heath wove his way through trees and underbrush, thankful the rain had softened the ground enough to muffle his movements. The men grew silent. With only the occasional sound of a shovel driven into the soft soil guiding him, he continued on his path. Reaching the edge of a cliff that overlooked a ravine with a creek down below, Heath paused, listening. He had to be close.

"That's it. I'm done!" came a shouted declaration to his right.

Heath ran in the direction of the voice.

"Shh. What was that?"

He darted behind a large oak tree, precariously close to the edge of the cliff, and pressed his back against the trunk.

"You're so paranoid. It's a deer or a squirrel or something."

"Yeah. Maybe."

"Who would be out there? We're not on the trail. And even if we were, do you really think anyone would be out hiking in this weather? Most likely, any through hikers are holed up at one of the shelters along the trail, waiting out the rain. And locals wouldn't be out for a hike on a day like this."

Peering around the tree, Heath spotted the two men. Dressed in camouflage, they stood in a small clearing with shovels in their hands. The younger man—redheaded, muscular, six foot four, late twenties—stood beside a partially dug grave, a body crumpled on the ground beside it. The older man—brown hair, husky, five foot ten, early to mid-thirties—threw down his shovel, picked up a rifle and walked straight toward Heath's hiding spot.

The man next to the grave dropped his shovel. "That's it. You stay out here and dig a grave if you want to, Joe. I'm going home."

"You can't do that, Larry!" The gun-carrying man spun and faced his companion. "We haven't buried the body yet."

"Of course I can." Larry drew himself to his full height. "I don't know how I let you rope me into this. I wasn't even there when you killed

Ray, so why do I care if they find his body? No one can tie me to his death."

Heath pulled out his cell phone and snapped a few quick photos before replacing it. Then he removed his Glock from its holster and waited, watching the scene unfold in front of him. He couldn't afford to rush too quickly and lose control of the situation.

"Where do you think you're going? You helped me transport the body across the state line. And if they trace his death back to me, *everything we've built* will come crashing down. You're in this as deeply as I am. Besides—" Joe softened his tone "—the grave's deep enough. All we gotta do is drop ol' Ray in and cover 'im up."

"Fine." Larry spat the word out. "But I'm not doing the work by myself."

"Deal." Joe leaned his rifle against a log and picked up the shovel he'd dropped earlier.

The younger man sighed. Then he bent, rolled the body into the open grave and picked up the other shovel.

Time for Heath to make his move. He eased around the tree and stepped out into the open. The men, engrossed in their task shoveling dirt on top of the body, were unaware of his presence. With his weapon trained on the men, he took two steps forward. "Hold it right there."

Both heads jerked upward and two pairs of eyes widened in disbelief.

"Who are you?" Joe growled, his face red, anger vibrating off him.

"Sheriff Dalton. And you're both under arrest." Heath jerked his head. "Put down the shovels and back away from the body."

The two men looked at each other. Larry nodded. Good. If the younger man would surrender, that would be half the battle.

Joe turned back to Heath, dropped his shovel, put his hands in the air, took one step backward and muttered something under his breath. Then Larry swung toward Heath and threw his shovel like a javelin. Heath stepped left. The sharp metal blade brushed past him. In his peripheral vision, he glimpsed Joe picking up the rifle.

Heath planted his feet, pivoted and lifted his arm, but Joe fired before he could pull the trigger. The bullet grazed his right arm. His gun flew out of his hand. He staggered backward and tumbled down the embankment toward the rocky ravine below.

*Lord, save me.*

Kayla Eldridge increased her wiper speed and leaned over the steering wheel to peer at the ominous sky. It seemed the weather wasn't any happier about her return to the Appalachian Mountains of Tennessee than she was. Why had she let Leslie talk her into accepting a one-month traveling nurse position here, of all places? *Be-*

*cause you wanted to spend time with your brother
and sister-in-law. And your sweet baby nephew.*
If Sawyer, Bridget and Vincent didn't live in Barton Creek, Kayla would never return to this part of Tennessee.

Her heart raced, her palms sweating.

*Breathe in...two...three...four...*
*Hold...two...three...four...*
*Release...two...three...four...*

Kayla heard her therapist as clearly as if she were sitting in the vehicle with her. Focusing on her breathing, she felt her anxiety ease a few degrees.

It was only for one month. She could handle anything for that amount of time. And it wasn't like she hadn't visited her family in the past four years. Her last visit was eighteen months ago, when Vincent had been born. Of course, that time, like every time before, she'd flown to Knoxville and someone had picked her up from the airport. She hadn't driven through the section of the region that tormented her dreams. Until now.

*Too late for remorse. You made a commitment
and you have to honor it.*

Suddenly, a dark-haired man burst out of the woods and into the road in front of her, waving his arm to flag her down. She slammed on the brakes and jerked her steering wheel. Her tires skidded on the slick pavement and her vehicle spun out of control, landing with a jolt, nose-first, in the ditch. The airbag exploded from the steering wheel in a puff of white.

Kayla coughed and waved her hand in front of her face, desperate to fan the dust cloud away from her eyes and nose. *What do I do now? Call Sawyer.* She reached across to the passenger seat for her purse. Not there. Unfastening her seat belt, she leaned as far as she could and felt around the floorboard. Her fingers connected with the leather strap and she tugged, pulling the purse to her.

The man banged on her driver's-side window. "Are you okay?" He pulled on her door handle. "Is the door locked? You need to get out of there."

"No." She shook her head. "I'll wait here. Until the police arrive." Kayla pulled her phone out of her purse. No service. Now what? What was the likelihood of another vehicle coming along and offering assistance? Slim to none. She had seen no one in the past twenty minutes.

The man banged on the door again. She turned to glare at him. He held an open wallet against the window, a police badge on display. Kayla leaned closer. Blount County Sheriff. She met his blue eyes. He closed one side of the wallet to display a driver's license. Heath Dalton. Her eyes widened. She'd heard Sawyer and Bridget mention his name. He was the youngest sheriff in Blount County history. According to Sawyer, he was also one of the best. Why was the sheriff in the middle of the road flagging her down?

"There's smoke coming out from under your vehicle," he said calmly. "If you think you can trust me now, I'd really appreciate you getting out. Just in case the car bursts into flames."

She gasped, draped her small cross-body purse strap over her head and opened her door. Sheriff Dalton reached for her hand. That's when she noticed his right arm hung by his side, blood on his sleeve. "You're injured."

"Just a scratch. Let's get a little distance between us and this car."

"Wait. I'm a nurse. Let me get my bag." Kayla crawled into her car, leaned way over the back of the front seat and snagged the backpack she had used as an overnight bag at the hotel along the route last night. Then she reached into the small duffel that held her nursing supplies, pulled out the smaller bag that held first-aid supplies and attached it to the carabiner that dangled from her backpack strap.

The sheriff took the pack from her. She climbed out of the car and ran with him across the road. They stopped beside a large boulder. Kayla looked over her shoulder at her vehicle. The smoke had dissipated. Relief washed over her. Her car hadn't caught on fire.

She turned to the man who'd caused the accident. "Why did you—"

"I'm sorry. Didn't mean to make you crash. As you can tell, I needed assistance and hoped to hitch a ride…"

Kayla lifted his right arm and he winced. "We need to get out of the rain so I can bandage your arm. We could go back to my vehicle."

"I'd rather not be in a confined space at the moment," he said as he scanned the woods behind them.

"Why? What are you not telling me?"

He looked around. "Have you met any vehicles on this road this morning?"

Kayla shook her head. "Not in the last twenty minutes or so."

"That's what I was afraid of. As much rain as we've had, fallen trees could have blocked the road or the bridge could have washed out."

"What are we going to do?" Fear rose inside her. *Please, not the woods. I can't go into the woods.* "It's about eight miles back to the last gas station. We can hike to it. Maybe a car will come along."

He sighed and pinned her with his gaze. "We can't stay on the road. It's too open. The men who did this—" Heath pointed to his arm "—are out there hunting me. If they spot us, we'll both be dead."

"Who's hunting you?"

"I don't know. I came upon two men burying a body. One of them shot at me—"

Kayla raised an eyebrow.

"Okay. He hit me, but the bullet only grazed my arm. I lost my balance and tumbled into the ravine. After I regained my wits, I headed due east, knowing I would eventually come out at this section of road. But I've caught sight of the men a few times, so I know they're still out there tracking me. The ravine runs parallel to the area where the men were digging, so I'm not surprised they were able to track me."

She looked him up and down. He wore nylon convertible pants, hiking boots and a rain jacket. And had the beginnings of a scruffy beard. He wasn't just out for a hike in the rain. "Where's your backpack?"

"I had to ditch it on the trail."

"And your gun?"

"Why would you think I'd carry a gun hiking?"

"Because I know lawmen. They don't go many places without their weapon."

"I lost my revolver. It flew out of my hand when the bullet hit me." He narrowed his eyes. "Okay, I've answered your questions. Now, you answer a few of mine. What's your name? Why do you *know lawmen*? And why are you out in this weather?"

"Kayla Eldridge. My brother is a former FBI agent."

"Sawyer Eldridge. I know him and his wife,

Bridget." The sheriff raised an eyebrow. "So, you're Kayla. The one who survived Lovelorn."

The mention of her former fiancé's serial killer name sent a shiver up her spine. Jonathan had completely fooled her. But he'd taught her love was an illusion and you should trust no one but yourself.

"Yeah, that's me. As for why I'm out driving in this weather..." She pointed at her first-aid kit that had an embroidered image of a stethoscope creating the shape of a heart with her first name in the center. "I'm a traveling nurse, and I've been assigned to Barton Creek Medical Center for a month."

The rain stopped and the clouds shifted, the sun peeking through for the first time all morning. Maybe it was an indication that things weren't as dreary as they seemed.

"Let me bandage your arm. Then you can go back into the woods and try to capture your criminals while I hike—on the road—to the gas station and call for help."

"I understand why you might have a fear of the woods, but I can't let you go off on your own. These men are dangerous. If they spot you, even if I'm not with you, you won't be safe. We need to stick together."

"Look, don't analyze my fears. I already have a counselor. I'm not looking for another one. And

I am absolutely not going into those woods, especially if there are killers on the loose."

"Hey, Joe," a gruff male voice yelled. "There's a car in the ditch."

Two men stepped out of the forest about fifty yards away. Heath grasped her hand and pulled her into the shelter of the trees. As they watched, the men crossed the road to her vehicle, the younger one climbing inside and looking around. The trunk popped open and the older man reached inside and opened one of her suitcases.

"They can't do that." She took a step, but Heath halted her, a finger to his lips.

The men looked in their direction, the older one lifting his rifle. A shot rang out. And a bullet hit the boulder where they had stood moments before.

Heath turned and ran, pulling her with him, deeper into the woods. Her heart pounding in her chest, Kayla ran as fast as she could, following Heath's movements as he wove in and out of trees. The gunmen were close behind. So much for her declaration that she wouldn't go into the woods. Now she simply had to figure out how to get out of them, alive, a second time.

# TWO

Pain radiated up his arm. Heath gritted his teeth. *Don't stop. Keep running.* Kayla stumbled, tugging his arm. He swallowed a gasp and slowed his steps. "Are you hurt?"

"No." She puffed out a breath. "What's the plan? I can't keep running indefinitely. Three miles is usually my limit, and I feel like we've far exceeded that."

He glanced over her shoulder. Surprisingly, both men were still there. He wouldn't have pegged Joe as being athletic. Thankfully, their pursuers were far enough behind them, Heath believed he could lose them. He'd seen a small fissure in the side of the mountain when he'd traveled this same trail earlier. If he could locate it again, maybe he could hide Kayla and lead the men away from her.

He'd never intended to get an innocent person involved in this mess. It was his job to protect the people in his county but right now he was failing miserably at that task. *Lord, don't let any-*

*thing happen to this young woman because of me. Please protect her.*

"Once we get around the curve up ahead, the trail will Y. We'll go right and hope they go left." Heath dropped her hand and slowed his pace, falling into step beside her. "Of course, they could decide to split up."

"Then what will we do?" Fear laced her words.

"I have a plan. You'll be safe. I promise."

She opened her mouth and then closed it with a slight shake of her head. He wished she wouldn't hold back her words, but he didn't know her well enough to tell her to be open with him.

They reached the Y, and he glanced back once more. The men weren't in sight. Sending up a silent prayer of thanks, he led the way. About half a mile past the Y, he saw the section of the mountain that had the jagged split. He hadn't spotted either man behind them since they'd switched trails, but it would be naïve to think one or both of the killers wasn't behind them, closing in.

Heath paused beside the fissure and turned to Kayla. She stopped and bent at the waist, holding her side.

"Thanks," she said, panting. "I needed a moment to catch my breath." She looked around. "How far back are they?"

"I haven't seen them since we turned on this trail, but I doubt they're far." He pointed to the opening in the rock face of the mountain. "It's narrow, but it looks deep. You can hide in the shadows. I'll lead them away."

"No." Kayla shook her head adamantly. "I'll stay with you."

"That's not a good idea. I'll be faster on my own. And you'll be safer here."

She straightened, pulled herself to her full height and locked eyes with him. "I won't stay here alone."

What was her problem? Didn't she understand he was trying to save her life? Her lower lip trembled. She captured it between her teeth. Realization hit like a bolt of lightning. Most people would be scared to be alone in the wilderness with killers on their trail, but for someone who had almost died—in a cabin in the woods—at the hands of a serial killer, the fear would be paralyzing. *What am I going to do, Lord? I don't have a weapon, and I'm not sure we can outrun these men.*

"Larry! I see fresh footprints. They went this way!"

How could Heath have forgotten about their footprints? The rain had stopped, so the prints weren't being washed away. He grasped Kayla by her shoulders and looked into her hazel eyes. Part of him wanted to beg her to stay put until he returned, but the only way to throw the killers off their trail would be with two sets of footprints continuing past this point. "I won't leave you. But we have to make them think we went beyond this point."

Heath quickly took in their surroundings. "There." He pointed to the smaller trail with thick underbrush he'd used earlier when he'd climbed out of the ravine. "We'll run straight up to that trail, stop on that mossy area and then quickly circle back, staying off the trail, on the grassy areas and rocks."

"Okay." She nodded and slipped her hand back into his, as if she was afraid that he would break his promise and leave her behind.

"Run!" he urged.

He bolted toward the side trail, Kayla keeping in step beside him.

"Stop!"

They pivoted on a thick carpet of moss. Then, as if they were playing a childhood game of hopscotch, they worked their way back to the hiding spot.

"Why are you going so slow?" Joe demanded.

"I was giving you a chance to catch up," Larry growled.

*Hurry,* Heath mouthed to Kayla and motioned for her to enter the crevice. He followed behind her. It would be a tight fit and he wasn't sure the shadows would completely hide both of them. *Don't let them find us, Lord.*

"Why? You have a gun," Joe declared as the men came into view.

"Would you just hurry up? They're going to get away."

Heath eased further into the fissure and felt Kayla grab a fistful of his jacket. He reached back and grasped her free hand. It had been a long time since he'd held hands with a woman as much as he had Kayla in only an hour. *It means nothing. You're just offering comfort in a diffi-cult situation. One you created by running into the road the way you did.*

"Nah. This trail leads to a dead end." Joe laughed and stopped to lean on a tree in clear sight of their hiding spot.

The subtle sound of Kayla sucking in her breath made Heath's heart skip a beat. He gave her hand a gentle squeeze, not taking his eyes off the men.

"How do you know that?"

"My dad brought me out here a lot as a child. His idea of punishment when I didn't toe the line was to make me hike for hours."

"So that's why you knew the sheriff would come out on the road where he did. You knew going the other way was a dead end."

"Well, yes, but also, I'm not directionally chal-lenged like you are. I knew the road was due east." Joe laughed.

Larry glowered, his face reddening to the same shade as his hair. "Yeah, well, I'm smarter than you in everything else and everyone in the family knows it."

So, the men *were* related. Larry didn't know about the hiking trips, so they probably weren't brothers. Maybe cousins. Or an uncle and nephew. Once Heath made it back to the station, he would send the photos he'd taken to local law enforcement agencies in North Carolina. The men had mentioned crossing the state line and Fontana Lake, which was in North Carolina.

"You know." Joe turned and started in the direction where Heath and Kayla hid. "When I was a kid, I'd hide from my dad in that crack in the mountain right there. He'd get so mad when he couldn't find me."

Kayla pressed against Heath's back, and he wondered if she might pass out from fear.

Larry grabbed the older man by the collar and halted him. "You're wasting time. We need to get to the end of this trail before they figure another way out."

"What if they're hiding in there?"

Heath reached for his weapon. Ugh. For a moment, he'd forgotten he'd lost it. Another example of the mistakes he'd made today. He needed to shake these guys and get back to the spot where he'd lost the Glock so he could locate it before someone else did.

"Do you really think two people would fit in there? Now, let's go."

The two men took off at a jog.

"When can we get outta here?" Kayla whispered, her breath tickling his neck.

He turned and banged his arm against the rock wall. He swallowed the scream of pain, involuntary tears stinging his eyes. "Soon," he said through gritted teeth.

"The footprints stopped!" Larry exclaimed. "Looks like they took this side trail. I thought you said this was a dead end."

"That's overgrown. How could they go that way?"

"Some of the weeds look pressed down, like someone recently went through them."

Heath hadn't thought about the weeds. He'd pushed them aside as he'd made his way through the thicket when he'd climbed out of the ravine. There was a nice carpet of clover along the section bordering the trail they were on, but once the men went farther down the side trail, it would become muddy. Would they see his solo footprints coming toward them, leading them back to the spot where he and Kayla hid?

"All I know is their footprints lead that way, ending here where the weeds are," Larry declared.

"Maybe they went back th—"

"Use your brain, Joe. Do you see any footprints going back that way? I'm sure they thought we'd miss this trail since there's so much overgrowth.

They have to be going slow to get through these briars. Come on, we'll catch them soon."

The men continued to argue, their voices growing quieter with each step they took away from their hiding place. Heath inched closer to the opening, Kayla glued to him every step of the way. The men had disappeared out of sight.

Heath put a finger to his lips and motioned for Kayla to follow him, then he stepped out into the daylight. They half-walked, half-jogged over the trail they'd traveled earlier. When they reached the Y, Heath turned right and Kayla turned left.

"Where are you going?" she asked. "We need to get out of the woods while they're roaming around in them looking for us."

"I have to go look for my gun. And I need to get pictures of the dead body for identification purposes." Heath pinched the bridge of his nose. His head hurt as much as his arm. "If you want to go back to the road, I can't stop you, but you'll be on your own if they find you."

Which would she be more afraid of, the woods with him or facing two killers alone? Heath knew he was putting her in a dangerous situation no matter which one she chose, but he hoped she'd stay by his side so he stood a chance of protecting her.

"Can't you come back later with some deputies to look for the body and your gun?" Kayla asked.

"That would cost too much time. In this weather, it will take a while to make it back to town. Your vehicle is out of commission, and even if we hike off the mountain, we may not be able to cross the bridge. The longer it takes to get a team out here to recover the evidence, the easier it will be for Joe and Larry to move the body and hide the evidence. Plus, it would be irresponsible for me to leave my weapon for someone to find." He shrugged. "The choice is yours. You do whatever you need to, but I've gotta go this way. It's my duty."

"What about your duty to protect me?" Kayla knew she sounded unreasonable even as the words came out of her mouth. A crime had been committed. The deceased person's family deserved answers. But she honestly didn't know how much deeper she could go into the woods.

"I *am* trying to protect you. If I have my way, we'll stay together. But, like I said, I can't stop you if you want to go your own way." Heath sighed. "Look, it won't take them long to figure out we're not on that trail. When they do, they're going to be after us. I can't wait around."

He turned and headed away from her. How could he be so calm? *He's law enforcement. He's trained to be that way.* The same as Sawyer. Was her brother aware of her disappearance yet? No, probably not. He didn't expect her to arrive at his house until dinnertime. Bridget had tried to get her to stay in their guest room. If only Kayla hadn't been determined to appear independent, she would have accepted the gracious offer. Instead, she'd rented a small cabin at the Hideaway Inn Bed and Breakfast. Now she had to choose between going deeper into the woods with a man she didn't know or facing the possibility of running into the men with guns. Alone.

Kayla puffed out a breath. "I'm coming." She ran after Heath. The woods were a dangerous place, with or without killers on the loose, and she couldn't traverse any portion of it on her own.

"I still need to dress your wound." Yeah, that was a good excuse for her to stick with him. "I'm guessing you won't let me do that until you find what you're looking for. However, you should know your risk of infection goes up the longer it's left untreated."

"Dually noted," he said and kept on walking.

"How do you know the way back to the body? Didn't you come out a different way after falling into the ravine?"

"I traveled a couple of miles along the creek bank at the bottom of the ravine then followed a trail up the side of the mountain and came out on the trail we were just on. The trail we're on now curves up ahead and runs parallel with the ravine. As long as we stay on it, I should be able to find the body."

"You seem to know a lot about these trails."

"Yeah, my dad took me and my brother camping each summer. This was his favorite spot close to home."

He reached for her backpack but she dodged his hand and went around him. She had to have some independence. "I've got this."

"Okay. If you insist." Heath fell into place beside her and they walked in silence.

With each step that carried them deeper into the woods, Kayla felt anxiety bubbling up inside her. She rubbed her palms on her legs. *Focus. Breathe. Pray.*

*Lord, I know You walk with me. You are my strength and my shield, and You will never leave me. Please, help me keep my anxiety at bay. I don't want to do anything to put Heath or myself in danger.*

Two hours later, Heath led them through a grove of trees and they came to small clearing.

"There's the grave," he exclaimed.

Kayla looked at the mound of dirt and her stomach lurched. She was going to be sick. Running to the nearest tree, she fell to her knees and heaved. Heath knelt beside her and brushed her hair back from her face. She turned away, wishing the ground would open up and swallow her whole. Even as a child, she hadn't liked for anyone to witness her retching. "Please, go away," she begged, her eyes burning with tears.

"I will, but…are you sure you're alright?"

Pressing her lips together, she nodded. Heat crept up her neck.

"Okay. But stay here while I get a look at the body. You don't need to see that." He walked away.

She settled into a seated position against the tree and buried her face in her hands. Unable to resist, she turned toward the grave and peered between her fingers. The last time she'd seen a grave that looked like this one had been in a photo of the grave of one of Jonathan's victims that Sawyer and Bridget had discovered on Bridget's grandparents' ranch. The prosecutor had showed the image at Jonathan's trial. Sawyer had tried to convince her not to attend every day of the trial and to only show up the day she was being called to testify. But she'd refused to miss a single day. As unbelievable as it might seem, she had needed to be in court to hear all of the horrible things Jonathan had done so that she could completely push him out of her heart.

"I told you not to look," Heath said as he shoveled dirt from the mound.

"I know... Where'd you find the shovel?"

"It was behind a bush. They didn't do too good of a job hiding it. Guess they were in a hurry to find me." He dropped the shovel and knelt beside the dirt pile, digging with his hands. "You may want to look away now."

She pushed to her feet and turned to face the

tree. "I can't stand here and do nothing. What if I look for your gun? Did you lose it somewhere around here?"

"I was just to the right of where you are now. It could be anywhere in the underbrush there." He grunted and she heard a scraping sound. "Don't look!"

She focused her eyes on the ground in front of her. "Is that the…?"

"Yes. He's facedown. I've got to roll him over and get photos. Then I'll replace him and cover him back up to protect the body from wild animals."

"I'll…uh…look around over here for your gun." She searched the underbrush near the tree, kicking leaves away with her feet. "Do you think it could have fallen into the ravine?"

"That's a possibility. It could have gone over when I did."

Kayla gasped and turned to stare at him, but the sight of a lifeless body had her quickly spinning back around. "*You* fell from this high up?"

"Yep."

She inched her way closer to the edge, peered into the ravine and scanned the area. This was harder than one of those find-the-hidden-object books she'd loved as a child. The gun could be anywhere. Too bad she couldn't pull out a magnifying glass like she had when the object she'd been looking for on the page had been especially tricky to find. Wait a minute. She pulled her cell phone out of her pocket. Maybe she could use the camera zoom.

Opening the app, she scanned the area, zooming a little more with each sweep of the lens. The gun wasn't anywhere in sight.

"Did you find it?" Heath spoke behind her.

She whirled around, lost her step and tipped backward. Heath caught her arm and pulled her forward. She slammed into his chest, his arms wrapping tightly around her. The sound of his heartbeat echoed hers, emphasizing how close she'd come to falling off the edge of the mountain. Another reminder that one wrong step and her life would be over.

The prayer she'd repeated over and over while being held hostage by Jonathan sprang to mind. *Lord, please don't let me die alone in the woods.*

She wasn't alone. But that fact didn't mean she wouldn't die this time.

# THREE

"I'm sorry," Heath whispered against her ear, his heart pounding in his chest. "I didn't mean to startle you." *Or myself.*

If she'd fallen over the edge, he had no idea what he would have done. It was going to be hard enough to face her brother after this was over. He didn't need to have to explain how he'd failed at protecting her while on the run from the killers.

Kayla stepped out of his arms and put some distance between them. "It's okay. I should have paid more attention to my surroundings. But I have a tendency to get absorbed in games."

"Games?"

"Yes." A sheepish smile crossed her face. "This would be a game of find-the-hidden-object."

"Like the *Where's Waldo* books?"

"Exactly."

"Did it work?"

"Not yet." She looked around him at the grave. "Did you finish?"

"I did. Now, I can look for my gun." Heath

shifted to block her view. He'd left the grave as he'd found it but didn't want to cause her more distress.

"I don't guess the…person…had any ID…"

"No. There wasn't a wallet or anything. That would have made things too easy."

"Why do you think they killed him?"

"I don't know, but I intend to find out." He cupped her elbow and guided her to the tree line. "Maybe my gun traveled farther than I thought. It could be in this thick underbrush."

"I'm not sure where that sheriff went." Joe's voice reached Heath's ears. He pulled Kayla deeper into the shadows of the trees. "But I guarantee you he'll be back here before nightfall looking for his gun."

Joe and Larry came into view on the other side of the clearing.

"Too bad for him. I already found it." Larry patted his jacket pocket.

Heath clenched his teeth and the muscle in his neck twitched. Not only had he lost his gun but it had fallen into the hands of a murderer.

"I'm sure he's on his way to town," Larry declared. "With all the flooding, it will take him longer to get there. I doubt he'll make it back out here tonight."

"Which is why we have to move the body. If they can't find it, they won't be able to tie the murder to us."

"But the sheriff and that woman saw us," Larry stated.

"And we'll take care of them. After we move our buddy here."

"We can't move him. It would take too long to find another place off the trail *and* dig another grave."

"Then what do you suggest?" Joe demanded.

Kayla moved closer to Heath. Her grip on his arm tightened, fear radiating from her. He wanted to comfort her but was afraid to move a muscle.

"We dig up some small plants, maybe a few wild hydrangeas or something similar, and plant them over the grave. They will hide the freshly dug dirt."

"That could work." Joe nodded thoughtfully. "Okay, grab a shovel and let's do this. Then we can make our way to Barton Creek and take care of the sheriff and the girl. It will be best for us if they aren't alive to identify us."

Heath turned to Kayla, his face inches from hers. "We need to get to higher ground so we can watch them without being spotted."

Her eyes widened and she nodded. There was no way he'd allow a woman, or any civilian, to be between him and men with guns. She'd have to go first and then he'd follow.

"Walk quickly and as lightly as you can. Stay straight. You'll come out on the trail. I'll be right behind you." He glanced over his shoulder. The men walked toward their hiding spot. "Go."

Kayla quickly made her way in the direction he had pointed, staying close to the trees. He followed her path. If they heard the men getting close, they could dart behind a tree for protection. Kayla was almost through the thicket of trees. Heath glanced back once more. As he did, he stepped on a small fallen branch and it snapped. He darted behind the closest tree, Kayla doing the same.

"What was that?" Joe demanded.

"I didn't hear anything," Larry replied. "Don't let your imagination run away with you. The sheriff doesn't have a weapon. He won't confront us in the woods."

A raccoon came out of a hollow log nearby and hissed. Larry laughed. "There's your boogeyman."

"Oh, hush, and start digging." The men returned to their task.

The raccoon glanced at Heath then went back into his den. *Thank you, little fella.* Heath turned his focus back to the tree where Kayla had taken shelter. There was no movement. *Good girl.* He prayed she stayed hidden until Larry and Joe left the wooded area.

Several long minutes later, the two men gathered the plants they'd dug and went back into the clearing. Heath slowly made his way to Kayla's hiding place.

"It's just me," he whispered as he drew near.

She peered around the tree and released a breath. "That was close."

"Yes, but they're in the clearing now. Let's get out of here."

They broke through the trees and came out on the trail. Even though Joe and Larry wouldn't be able to see them from their vantage point now, Heath wouldn't feel completely at ease until they had put more distance between themselves and the killers.

"I left my camping gear over here." He crossed to the thicket of shrubs and pulled his backpack out of its hiding place. He gingerly slipped his injured arm through the strap, gritted his teeth and secured the pack on his shoulders. Then he fastened the chest strap and waist belt before turning to face Kayla. She wore her own small backpack with the first-aid kit attached to it with a carabiner. "Do you want me to carry some of that?"

Now why had he asked that? With his injury, he could barely handle the weight of his own pack.

"No. I can manage." She straightened to her full height, as if daring him to contradict her.

Heath hadn't meant to insinuate she wasn't able to carry a backpack or take care of herself. His mom had raised him to be a gentleman. Offering to help a lady was instinctive. "Okay, let's go before they discover us here."

Hiking at a brisk pace, he led the way further into the woods. Away from the ranger station where he had parked his vehicle. They would have to take the Crooked Falls trail. It was a strenuous trail, more suited for advanced hikers, but he didn't see that they had a choice if they wanted to go around the killers and reach the ranger station. The only problem was it would take them longer to hike that trail, which would mean camping in the woods overnight. Heath wasn't sure how he would break the news to his companion. Hopefully, he'd figure it before time to set up camp.

Kayla wasn't sure which ached more, her back or her feet. They had taken another trail and had been going steadily uphill for at least half a mile. If she'd known she was going hiking when she'd dressed this morning, she would have worn something with a little more support than her canvas sneakers. At least she had some thick socks in her backpack. Once they stopped to treat Heath's wounds, she'd change into them. They would provide a little more padding to her poor feet.

"You said we were going to higher ground so we could watch what they're doing. Is that still the plan? I can't see them from here."

"It's not much farther." Heath moved a dangling briar out of the way and motioned for her to pass under it.

"We've been walking for twenty minutes. Aren't you afraid they'll be gone before we get to this, um, viewing location?"

The trail widened and he slowed and fell into step beside her, taking the side closest to the edge, which she'd noticed him doing several times. He seemed the perfect Southern gentleman. Of course, she knew better than anyone that people could appear to be good on the outside and be pure evil on the inside. Not that she thought Sheriff Heath Dalton wasn't a hundred percent one of the good guys.

After finding out she would be in Barton Creek for several weeks, Bridget had hinted—not too subtlety—that she wanted to introduce Kayla to the young, handsome sheriff. Kayla had quickly informed her sister-in-law that she wasn't looking for a romantic relationship. It had taken her years to work through the trauma of almost dying at the hands of her fiancé, Jonathan Smith. A serial killer dubbed "Lovelorn" by the press, who'd murdered eleven women and had only used Kayla to get to her brother Sawyer—a former FBI profiler who'd stopped Jonathan from killing his prized target eighteen months prior.

Some years ago, Kayla had read an article that estimated the number of killers a person unknowingly walked past in their lifetime to be thirty-six. The two men today brought the total number of murderers who had attempted to kill her to three. She shuddered. Maybe she should move to a remote island and live a life of solitude. If she survived this latest attempt on her life.

"Are you cold?" Heath caught her hand and halted her. "I have a sweatshirt in my backpack. Give me a second to dig it out."

Kayla waved him off. "I'm fine. I just let my thoughts wander a little too far into the past. That's all."

"Do you want to talk about it? I'm a good listener."

"Thank you, but…no."

He smiled, a half smile that didn't reach his eyes. One most people smiled when they sensed the situation didn't warrant a smile but they wanted to give some form of support.

"If you change your mind, the offer will stand." He pointed to a rocky area that jutted out over the valley below. "There's our viewing spot."

It was beautiful. If she'd found this site at any other time, and at a location that wasn't deep in the woods, she would have wanted to stop and take pictures and maybe watch the sunset.

"Come on." Heath led her over to a boulder that had a flat surface on top. "Let me climb up first. Then I'll help you."

"Okay."

He scaled to the top of the rock, shrugged off his backpack and then reached out to her. She slipped her hand into his and a jolt of awareness zinged up her arm. No, not awareness. It was static electricity. That's all. Kayla exhaled a deep breath and climbed onto the large rock, Heath's hand keeping her from falling.

Reaching the top, she dropped her backpack next to his and took a moment to enjoy the view. It was breathtaking.

"Look. There." Heath came up beside her and pointed to an area down below.

She sucked in a breath. They were almost directly above the location where the killers had buried the body. The dirt mound was now covered with plants and shrubs. It still looked like a grave to her, but she didn't know if someone who hadn't already seen it as a grave would know it was one.

"I don't see the men. Larry and Joe?" She looked at the man beside her. "How do you know their names?"

"I heard them having a conversation as I came upon their crime scene." He walked over to his backpack and pulled out a pair of binoculars. "I stayed hidden and listened long enough to figure out who was who. Then I snapped a few pictures of them with my camera for evidence, since

I didn't have cell service and couldn't get deputies here quickly."

"There's no cell service anywhere on the trail?"

"This deep in the woods, with all the mountains, it's hit or miss." Heath put the binoculars to his eyes.

*It's hit or miss.* This location was the highest point they had been all day. She pulled out her phone and sat on the rocky surface. The little bars at the top of the screen indicated the phone had a weak cell signal. She didn't want to end up in a game of phone tag with Sawyer, not on something this important. But maybe she could get a text message through to him.

Had an accident.

No, that wouldn't do. She deleted what she'd written and started over.

Cell service is spotty. I'll explain everything later. Wrecked my vehicle, but I'm fine. I'm with Sheriff Dalton. We are on...

"What's the name of this trail we're on?"

"Crooked Falls," he answered without taking his attention away from his search for the men. "Why?"

"I'm sending Sawyer a text telling him the situation."

"What?" He turned to her. "You have cell service."

"It's not great." Crooked Falls hiking trail, she typed as she talked. "May not work but worth a shot." Had to escape armed men.

Kayla chewed on her lower lip. She didn't want to worry Sawyer. There wasn't anything he could do about the situation. Maybe she should delete the last line. "Should I tell him about Larry and Joe?"

Heath furrowed his brow. "Wouldn't serve any purpose at the moment, other than worrying him. With the floodwaters in the valley, help can't reach us before tomorrow. Just tell him we'll be camping at Foster Point tonight and we—"

"What?" Now it was her turn to be surprised. "No. I can't spend the night in the woods. There's no…" Her hands shook and she released a quivering breath.

Heath knelt beside her. "I know this is hard for you. Sawyer hasn't disclosed all the details of your…ordeal. But I know enough to understand your fears. Believe me, if there was any way I could get you out of here tonight, I would. But I promise you won't be alone. I'll protect you. Tell Sawyer we'll meet him at the ranger station tomorrow afternoon. Around five."

"That's twenty-four hours from now."

"I know."

She bit her lower lip and nodded.

Camping at Foster Point tonight. Meet us at the ranger station tomorrow afternoon. We'll be there by five. Don't worry.

She hit Send. Then quickly added, I love you all!

"Did you see Larry and Joe?"

"Not yet." Heath stood and gave her a hand up. "I want to look one more time, then we'll be on our way."

He turned back to his search, peering through his binoculars. The men could be anywhere.

"I still need to clean your wou—" Her cell phone rang, drowning out the rest of her words. She gasped and looked at the screen. Sawyer. Swiping her finger across the screen to answer, she put the phone to her ear. "Sawyer? Can you hear me?"

"Kayla, why are you on a hiking trail and who are the men with guns?"

What? She closed her eyes and sighed. She'd forgotten to delete that part from the message. "It's okay we lost them."

"They found us!" Heath exclaimed.

He held the binoculars to her eyes. Larry and Joe stared up at them. The men took off running through the thicket of trees she and Heath had used earlier as an escape route. Her eyes widened.

"Did Heath say they found you? Kayla, answer me!" Sawyer demanded.

This was her fault. She was the one who'd given their location away. If she hadn't sent a text to Sawyer or if she had turned off the ringer... The weight of guilt settled on her shoulders. She had done it again. She had put herself—and another—in danger because of her carelessness.

# FOUR

Heath shoved the binoculars into his backpack. Then, picking up the pack, he dropped it to the ground beside the boulder where they stood and turned to Kayla, holding out his hand for her phone. Relief momentarily crossed her face as she placed it in his hand.

He pressed the phone to his ear, watching as she picked up her bags and dropped them beside his. "Sawyer, I'll explain everything once we're out of these woods."

Kayla sat, dangled her feet over the side of the boulder and slipped to the ground below. And then quickly shrugged into her backpack.

"How did my sister end up on the hiking trail with you?" Sawyer demanded.

There would be many questions once this ordeal was over and Heath would answer every one of them. But not now. "Parker can tell you where I left my truck. Meet us there in twenty-four hours… Oh, arrange for someone to pick up

Kayla's vehicle once the roads are passable. I'll text you where to find it."

"Don't dismiss me, Heath! That's my sister with you."

"And I'm trying to keep her, and myself, alive. The longer I stand around chatting, the closer the killers get to us. Sorry, but we have to go." He disconnected the call, sent a quick text telling Sawyer the location of Kayla's car and turned the phone off. Then he mimicked the move he had witnessed Kayla perform earlier and landed beside her.

Determination had replaced the fear he had seen in her eyes earlier. She seemed resolved with the situation they found themselves in. This was a good sign. If she was panicking, it would be harder to make progress. Hopefully, she would follow instructions so they could keep what little lead they had. And the killers wouldn't catch up to them.

Slipping his uninjured arm through the shoulder straps on his backpack, he slung it over his shoulder. Kayla raised an eyebrow. He wasn't hiding anything from her. And he knew his wound needed treated, but it would have to wait a little longer.

"Are you ready?" Heath searched her face.

"Do I have a choice?" she queried, a stony mask slipping into place over her facial features.

Being resolved to the situation didn't equate to

being happy with it. Heath sighed. He'd looked forward to meeting Sawyer's sister after hearing that she was coming to Barton Creek. This hadn't been the introduction he'd expected. Sawyer's wife, Bridget, had hinted at having him over for dinner. He suspected she'd planned to play matchmaker. Of course, he would have discouraged any such idea. But he had great respect for Sawyer and Bridget and had heard many stories about the ordeal they had endured while tracking Lovelorn. Sawyer had spoken with pride about his sister. How she'd overcome the near-death experience and become a nurse, living her life in service to others. Kayla was an impressive woman. Heath had hoped they could be friends. He doubted that would be possible now. Once he got her to safety, she would probably never want to see him again. And he couldn't blame her.

When his girlfriend, Erin, had broken up with him three years ago, she had told him his chosen career did not lend itself to him having healthy relationships—neither friendship nor romantic. That was probably why he only had a few close friends. Two of whom were happily married former law enforcement officers. The key term being *former*. Their careers had been over, or were coming close to the end, when they'd each met the woman they would marry.

Heath had known juggling a relationship and career in law enforcement would be tricky. After all, he'd seen the toll his father's career in law enforcement had had on his parents' relationship. But even though there had been occasions when his dad couldn't be at school and sporting events, or he'd had to miss a wedding anniversary—and there had been a short time when it seemed they might get a divorce—Heath's parents had worked through the difficulties and ultimately built a strong marriage that they were enjoying as they entered their retirement years.

Though his parents had overcome the difficult times, when he was a teenager, Heath had declared that he never wanted to fall in love. It was his childhood dream to be in law enforcement, and he didn't want to risk going through the struggles he'd witnessed his parents deal with through the years. Then he'd met Erin and fallen for her. When she had broken up with him, he'd been reminded of his resolution to remain single.

Heath loved his job and felt it an honor to be the sheriff of his county, especially at only thirty-four years of age. He didn't foresee retiring from law enforcement for at least thirty years. And when he did, he was sure he'd be even more set in his ways and live his remaining years as a hermit.

Leading the way, Heath took off up the trail, Kayla keeping pace with his stride. He wasn't sure how long they could keep going at such a fast pace before she'd need a break. He could only hope the men following them would also tire easily and stop more often than they did.

Thirty minutes later, the clouds parted and the setting sun shined straight into their faces. Lifting his hand, Heath shielded his eyes and blinked to clear the spots from his vision. "Once we top this ridge and head down the other side, the sun should shift enough that it's not shining in our eyes."

"How much farther until we can stop for a few minutes?" Kayla winced. "Sorry. I didn't mean for that to sound snippety. I'm sure you're tired, too."

"Yes, but unlike you, I'm dressed for hiking." He looked at her feet. "You're going to have blisters."

"I know." She sighed. "I had planned to put on a pair of thick socks when we stopped at the overlook, but then…"

"Sawyer called and gave away our location."

"That was my fault, not his. I'm the one that told him armed men were hunting us." She frowned and a tear escaped from the corner of her eye and slid down her cheek.

He'd never enjoyed seeing women cry. Given a choice, Heath would normally slip away and not return until he knew they had composed themselves. In this instant, a stronger urge to wrap Kayla in his arms and hold her until she released all of her pent-up anger and fear had replaced the urge to flee. Heath sensed she wouldn't welcome such a display of concern. More than likely, she'd mistake his compassion for pity.

Guilt washed over him and a wave of if-onlys hit him full force. If only he hadn't allowed the killers to get the jump on him... If only he hadn't lost his gun... If only he hadn't run into the road and caused Kayla to crash...

*Lord, please, let me get Kayla out of these woods alive. She's been through so much already. I can't let her down.*

*You're out for a springtime stroll. God's beauty surrounds you. Fresh air and exercise are good for the soul.* Kayla swallowed the sigh that threatened to escape. No amount of positive thoughts could make her forget she was deep in the wilderness with a man she didn't know, trying to stay ahead of the killers tracking them.

If—no, not if, when—when she got out of this situation, she would call the supervisor at the clinic and give her apologies that she was unable to fulfil her commitment. Then she would go straight back to Virginia and get a permanent job in a doctor's office or hospital. Her mom would love to have Kayla stay put in one place, especially close to her.

Kayla would live the most cautious life she could. Buy a condo a few miles from her mom and not venture too far from home. If she got lonely, she'd adopt a cat from a shelter. Many people lived happy lives alone with a pet for companionship. She could, too.

"This looks like a good place to stop and rest for a bit." Heath broke into her thoughts.

She looked around. They'd reached a small grove of trees and a fallen log partially blocked their path.

Heath pulled a poncho out of his backpack and spread it over the log. "Hopefully, this will keep you somewhat dry while you change your socks."

"Thanks. I also need to dress your wound."

"That can wait."

"No, it can't." She pinned him with a stare. "It's already been too long. I won't move another inch until I've treated you."

He opened his mouth then closed it and nodded. "Okay. Tend to yourself first, while I climb to higher ground to see if I can spot Joe and Larry. Then you can treat my wound."

Kayla watched as he slipped the binoculars over his head, grabbed a low-hanging limb, grimaced and swung into a tree. When he'd said *climb*, she had thought he'd meant take a trail to the top of the hill the base of the fallen log rested against. But he had actually meant climb a tree. In spite of his injury, he quickly disappeared into the treetop, the leaves offering a decent amount of camouflage.

Digging into her backpack, she pulled out the

thick pair of purple fleece-lined socks she slept in to keep her perpetually cold feet warm at night. Then she opened her small duffel and retrieved the first-aid kit. Slipping out of her shoes, she peeled off her wet socks and quickly dabbed antibacterial ointment on the red-blistered spots. Next, she covered them with Band-Aids and then slipped her feet into the warm dry socks.

Leaves rustled and she looked up just in time to see Heath drop to the ground. He dusted his hands off and turned to her. "I couldn't see them."

"What does that mean?" She loosened the strings on her Converse, shoved her feet into them, silently grimacing at the pinched feeling around her toes, and quickly tied them.

"It means they're at least ten minutes behind us, maybe more. Either way, we need to get moving."

"After I treat your wound." She stood and nodded to the log. "Have a seat."

"Are you always so stubborn?" he asked as he shrugged out of his jacket.

"Only when it comes to people's health and well-being."

Kayla gently rolled back the sleeve on his shirt, the dried blood causing it to tug at his skin. Heath scowled. She hadn't expected so much blood. He'd said the bullet had grazed him. This might be worse than she'd expected.

"Is hiking something you do often?" Kayla

asked, trying to distract him as she dug in her duffel for a small bottle of saline.

"Not really. The last time I went camping was three years ago when my brother Parker was home on leave."

"So what brought you into the woods this time? Alone." She generously applied the saline to his sleeve and the blood loosened, allowing her to push the fabric above the wound.

"Parker opened a camping store. He asked me to test some of the gear for him."

There were two wounds on Heath's upper arm. One looked like a burn that started as a solid mark and then split into two marks, the space in between unharmed. It looked almost identical to the image of a gunshot graze she'd seen on a teen gang member while completing college clinicals. Right above the burn was a gash, three inches long and half an inch deep. That's where the blood had come from. "How did you get the cut? The bullet wouldn't have done it."

He craned his neck to look at his arm. "Hmm. I guess Larry hit me with the shovel. I thought he missed. Of course, Joe shot at me at the same time."

"You were *hit* with a shovel blade *and* shot?" This was not good.

"Yeah. Larry threw the shovel like a javelin. I attempted to dodge it when Joe shot at me."

"Well, it looks like you didn't dodge either of

them." She leaned closer. The area around the cut was red and inflamed. Lifting a hand, she touched his arm.

He jerked. "Oh, your hands are cold."

She touched the back of her hand to her cheek. "Actually, they're not. Your wound is feverish. It should have been cleaned hours ago."

Holding his arm out, she poured the entire contents of the bottle of saline over the wound, doing her best to clean all the debris from the cut. Kayla applied a generous amount of antibiotic ointment over the cut and the bullet burn. Then she closed the wound with three butterfly closures and wrapped his upper arm with gauze.

"You'll have to keep this dry. The cut really should have had stitches. But this is the best I can do out here. I'll change the bandage again in the morning." She returned her supplies to her bag and pulled out a bottle of pain reliever. "Take two of these. It will help with the fever and should ease the pain."

He accepted the two capsules and quickly swallowed them.

"Thank you. I appreciate you taking the time to treat my wound." Heath stood. He picked his jacket up off the log and slid his hands through the sleeves. "I'm sorry I put you in this situation."

"You've already apologized. No need to do it again." She put everything back into her duffel.

He caught her hand and met her gaze. "Agreed.

But only if you stop apologizing about the phone call. You've done so several times and you have absolutely nothing to be sorry for."

"Deal."

A low growl sounded behind Heath. The hairs on the nape of Kayla's neck stood on end. She leaned slightly and looked behind him.

"What is it?" Heath asked under his breath.

She licked her lips. "Coyote."

"Okay. Stay…still. I'll try to scare it away." He slowly straightened, his body blocking her from the wild animal.

She met his eyes and dug inside her duffel. Her hands connected with her key ring. She clutched it tightly, praying the keys wouldn't jingle, pulled it out and held her palm open. "I have a personal security alarm and pepper spray. Will they help?"

He raised an eyebrow and took the oversize key ring with all the safety gadgets Bridget and Sawyer had given her for the first birthday she'd celebrated after her abduction. Kayla had nervously laughed when she'd opened the gift and had silently prayed she'd never need to use it. Thankfully, she hadn't. Until now.

"Everything I've read says to make yourself appear bigger than the animal to scare it away. But pepper spray can't hurt." He unsnapped the leather pouch that attached the small cylinder to the key ring and slid it out. A deeper growl sounded from the animal. "Okay, here goes."

He turned and stretched to his full height. "Go! Get outta here!" he bellowed and clapped his hands.

The coyote crouched and goose bumps popped out on Kayla's arms. Heath lifted his hand and released a stream of pepper spray. The animal yelped and backed up several feet, his teeth bared.

Fear froze Kayla in place. The animal didn't appear to be fazed. What were they going to do? A breeze blew through the trees and the remnants of the pepper spray drifted over Kayla. Her eyes burned. Covering her mouth and nose, she folded over in a fit of coughs. The coyote barked and she straightened in time to see him lunge at Heath, who had turned to check on her.

Grasping the small safety alarm attached to her key ring, Kayla pulled the pin at the same instant Heath released a second stream of pepper spray. The tiny alarm emitted a piercing sound as a flashing light strobed in the late-afternoon sunlight. She dropped the device and quickly covered her ears. The coyote howled and took off running in the opposite direction.

Heath picked up the key ring and replaced the pin in the device, halting the obnoxious noise. She cautiously lowered her hands, her ears still ringing. "Is he gone?"

"Yes. I imagine he's in the next county by now." Heath stuck his fingers in his ears and then pulled them out again. "I knew those things were loud, but wow, I hope it doesn't cause permanent hearing damage."

"Sor—"

"Uh-uh." He lifted his pointer finger and wiggled it. "Remember, no more apologizing. You did what you had to do to keep us safe. But now..." He looked down the trail they had traveled to this point. "We need to get moving. I'm not sure the killers can pinpoint our location from that siren, but I don't want to stick around and find out."

Kayla quickly shoved everything into her duffel, zipped it and shrugged into her backpack. "Let's go."

Heath extended a hand and helped her to her feet. They went around the log and took off at a pace that would rival any speed-walking champion. Kayla's eyes shifted from the ground to the trail ahead as she worked to remain upright and not trip over a rock or root. At least the sun had shifted in the sky and no longer blinded her as they continued their trek westward on the trail.

She prayed they could stay ahead of the men. The pepper spray and alarm may have worked against a wild animal, but she doubted they would work against men with guns.

# FIVE

It was getting dark. They needed to find a place to rest for the night. The trail was treacherous enough in daylight, no need to make it even more dangerous by hiking without proper light. Heath had a headlamp, but was hesitant to use it without knowing how much distance was between them and the men tracking them.

They'd passed the campsite he'd wanted to stay at overnight a mile back. It wouldn't be safe to set up camp in a location where Joe and Larry could stumble upon them. Heath had been on this trail with Parker once years ago, when his brother had been home on leave. If he remembered correctly, there was a cave nearby. If he could locate it, they could rest in a warm, dry place for the night.

"Are you still making it okay?" he asked over his shoulder.

"I'm fine."

Kayla hadn't complained once, but he'd seen her feet when she'd put on the thicker socks. She had to be in a great deal of pain. Add to that the strenuous exercise from the hike. Even if she was someone who exercised regularly, he was sure she'd be sore for days.

"There's a cave about a quarter of a mile further. Do you think you can make it that far?"

"Yes," came the single-word response.

He suspected she'd been silently berating herself for setting off the alarm earlier, though he'd told her he would have done the same thing. If she hadn't scared off the coyote, the killers would have found their mangled bodies and been happy they could save a couple of bullets. Either way, he and Kayla would both be dead if it hadn't been for her quick actions. Why couldn't she see that?

The sound of running water reached his ears. He slowed his pace and fell in beside her. "Do you hear that?"

She cocked her head. "Water."

"We're getting close to the waterfall. There are two streams we'll have to cross before we reach the end of the trail. The waterfall forms one of them."

"We're not crossing it tonight, are we?"

"No. But since we can hear the water, it means the cave is nearby." He shrugged out of his backpack and dropped it against an enormous oak tree. "Find a spot to sit and rest while I scout the woods and look for it."

Fear flashed in her eyes. "Is that a good idea?

To separate? What if the men show up? Or another coyote?" she asked in rapid succession.

He placed his hands on her shoulders. "I'm not going far. And I won't be gone long. If I don't find the cave quickly, we'll move on down the trail a little further."

She bit her bottom lip and nodded.

Heath pulled her into an embrace and hugged her tightly. "I'll stay within earshot. All you have to do is whistle." He smiled. "Or trigger that deafening alarm."

Kayla giggled and pushed him away. "If you're gone too long, I just might do that." A frown dropped into place. "Please, hurry."

*Lord, why does it feel like I'm abandoning her by leaving her here while I walk a few dozen yards away?*

He dropped his hands and took off without looking back. The sooner he found the cave, the sooner he'd be able to return for her.

If he was correct, the cave was a short distance up the side of the mountain. The hike to it hadn't been difficult, but locating the trail at the base had been because of the trees. That was another reason the cave would be a good place to hide for the night. The sun dipped behind the mountain. He had to hurry if he wanted to find the cave and get Kayla into it before it was too dark to see.

The trail came into view. It had overgrown with weeds since his last visit, but it was still passable. Now, to make sure there weren't any wild animals lurking around the cave before he went back to get Kayla. Would she be okay with the accommodations, considering he wouldn't be able to build a fire to light the interior?

Guilt washed over him. He pushed out a slow breath. She had been a trooper during their entire hike today, even when fear had been evident on her face. So, she wouldn't complain, no matter how uncomfortable or scary the sleeping arrangement might be.

He jogged the remaining distance to the cave opening, his steps faltering as he drew near. A large oak tree had fallen across the opening, completely blocking it. Clenching his teeth, he tamped down his frustration, spun and raced down the side of the mountain, not stopping until he reached Kayla.

She jumped to her feet. "What is it? What's wrong?"

A cramp stabbed his side. He bent, huffing out air. "A tree...blocking the...cave..." He straightened and released one more slow breath of air. "We'll have to find another place to set up camp."

"Okay." Kayla nodded, her eyes round.

Heath picked up his backpack and slipped it on once more, trying to ignore the concern he saw in her eyes. He *would* find a place for her to rest. "Where to now?"

An idea struck. When he and Parker had hiked

this trail, they'd walked behind the waterfall. He vaguely remembered a recessed area that would hide them from view. "How do you feel about sleeping under a waterfall?"

"I'm not sure. Do you think we'll encounter other wild animals?"

"I don't think so, but I can't promise we won't."

She shrugged. "Oh well, I don't guess we really have a choice. Lead the way."

Once this ordeal was over, he owed this strong, determined woman a nice, relaxing dinner at the finest restaurant. Not a date. A *thank you* between friends.

The waterfall came into view as the last colorful streaks of the sunset disappeared below the horizon. Heath was in awe of God's beauty. Even with evil lurking in the dark, the Light of the world would always be close.

"Beautiful. Something only God could create," Kayla observed as if she'd read his mind.

"Absolutely. Come on." He clasped Kayla's hand and led her behind the shrubs that hid the open side of the waterfall.

Darkness had settled like a blanket around them, making it difficult to see where to step. Kayla stubbed her toe on a root and tumbled forward. Heath turned and caught her.

"Hang on." He pulled the headlamp off his head and placed it on hers. Then he turned it on the lowest beam. "We can't leave it on long, but hopefully Larry and Joe are far enough back that it won't hurt to use it a few minutes."

She reached up and adjusted the band, her hair scrunching up around it.

Heath gently smoothed her hair. She smiled up at him. *What would it be like to kiss her lips?*

He dropped his hands and stepped back. "I'll turn on my phone light." He dug his cell phone out of his back pocket and activated the flashlight app.

"Do you think they're close enough to see?" she whispered.

Heath could almost feel the fear zinging through her body. He captured her hand once more and laced his fingers with hers, praying she'd take comfort knowing he was there to protect her. "I hope not."

Leading, he continued working his way through the underbrush until they reached the opening behind the waterfall. They climbed a small section of rock and reached a dirt ledge that was about twelve feet deep and ran the width of the waterfall. The rock ceiling above them was maybe ten feet tall at its highest and tapered to three feet as it neared the back of the ledge.

He shined his light over the area. There was a small alcove tucked behind a wall of rock to their left that seemed to be protected from view. Not that he expected Larry and Joe to walk behind the waterfall while they slept. If they made it to this point, they would most likely cross to the other side where the creek narrowed and there were large rocks they could use to hopscotch across the water. Or at least that was Heath's prayer.

Kayla shrugged out of her backpack and dropped it on the dirt floor of their abode for the night. She knew she should be thankful to have a place to rest, but the thought of the killers—or wild animals—stumbling upon them while they had their guard down made her skin crawl. There would be no way she'd get any sleep. It would be a repeat of the first night she'd spent locked in the cabin with the bomb strapped to her. Afraid to move a muscle, she had sat frozen in place, wide awake, for thirty-six hours before she'd finally become so physically exhausted she'd dozed off for a few hours. Then the cycle had repeated itself. *Then Sawyer showed up and saved you.* Only, her big brother couldn't save her this time. Even if he could reach her, she didn't want him putting his life on the line for her again. He had a wife and a child, and they needed him.

"I thought we could set up behind this rock wall," Heath said, breaking into her thoughts. He turned off the flashlight app and shoved his phone into his pocket. "We still need to be careful with the light, but I think it will be fine to use the headlamp, since it is set on the lowest setting. At least long enough to eat and get everything arranged."

"Okay. What can I do to help?"

He dug into his backpack and pulled out a sleeping bag and a tent. No, not a tent.

"Is that a hammock?" She raised an eyebrow.

"Yeah. It's a camping hammock, designed to take the place of a tent." He stretched it out on the ground. "Unfortunately, it doesn't work if you don't have trees to hang it. But I thought we might use it to block the mist, especially any water that sprays out if the wind blows."

Kayla frowned. Did he expect them to huddle under the nylon fabric together?

"What's wrong?" Heath asked.

"Oh, sorry." She bit her lip. Her face had betrayed her thoughts, as usual.

"Please, tell me what's on your mind," Heath prodded.

"I… We… I know there are more pressing issues, but to be honest, it's awkward…" She swept her hand toward the small alcove.

"Oh. Right." He rubbed his cheek. "How about this? I'll unzip the sleeping bag and spread it out. You take the side next to the wall, then we'll stack the backpacks in the middle, and I'll take the side closest to the opening."

Her heart smiled. His suggestion reminded her of one of those old black-and-white movies from the 1940s. He really was a good guy. "Thank you.

But if Larry and Joe show up, I'm not sure I want to be trapped behind backpacks." She sighed out a breath. "It will be okay. I'm being ridiculous."

"No. You're not." He bent down and spread out the fully unzipped sleeping bag. "Take your bags and get settled. I need to capture some water in the hydration reservoir bag and treat it so it's potable."

He sprinted to the waterfall and filled the water container. Kayla scooted her bags to the back of the alcove and sat on the sleeping bag. Digging inside her backpack, she took out the small, fuzzy, throw blanket that she always traveled with and wrapped it around her body. The temperature in the small cave behind the waterfall was noticeably cooler.

A loud rumbling noise emanated from her stomach. She crossed her arms over her middle as heat radiated up her neck and cheeks.

"I heard that," Heath said from the alcove opening. She could practically hear the smile in his voice.

"Yeah, it's been a while since breakfast." Kayla bit her lower lip. She knew she could survive days without food, having gone over seventy-two hours without food or drink when Jonathan had left her in the cabin, but it didn't mean she wanted to do so again. Did she have any snacks in her bag? Maybe gum.

Settling on the ground beside her, Heath unzipped his pack. "I hadn't planned on having any more meals on the trail after this morning, so I don't have a lot of food. But I packed an extra day's worth of supplies in case something happened and my plans had to change." He pulled out a couple of protein bars, beef jerky and a small bag of trail mix. Then he reached in again and came out with a pouch of freeze-dried stew. "We can't risk building a fire, but I guess if we have to, we can eat this cold tomorrow."

"It looks like a feast to me." She accepted a protein bar. "Thank you."

"It's probably time to turn off the light. Are you all settled?"

*No!* She wanted to plead with him to leave the light on. Four years, seven months and thirteen days. That's how long it had been since Kayla had slept in a room without some light. Right after her attack, she hadn't been able to sleep unless she'd had the bedroom light and the TV on. Then Sawyer had recommended a therapist to help her work through her trauma and, six months later, she could turn the light off but still left the TV on all night. Finally, a year ago, she'd been able to transition to a night-light that cast a faint glow and no longer needed the television to light the room. Dr. Clarke had been trying to get her to give up the security of the night-light for a while now. Ready or not, it looked like tonight would be the night she finally faced the dark.

"Kayla? Are you okay?"

She swallowed and removed the headlamp. "Yes."

He accepted the headlamp and turned off the light. Then he reached across and clasped her hand. "I'm here. I won't leave you."

Tears stung her eyes. Was he always so compassionate or was he simply being nice because he knew about her trauma?

"How much has Sawyer told you?"

"About your abduction? Not much. I was working in Nashville when Sawyer captured Lovelorn—"

"His name is Jonathan. Jonathan Smith." Now why had she said that? Was she trying to make him sound more likeable? No, that wasn't it. No matter what he was called, Jonathan, aka Lovelorn, would always be associated with his evil deeds.

"When I accepted a job as a deputy in Barton Creek a few weeks after *Jonathan* was captured, the entire town was talking about him and his victims." He squeezed her hand. "After I got to know Sawyer, I eventually mustered the courage to ask him a few questions about the case. All he said was you and Bridget suffered because of him. And that no one should ever have to go through what you did."

She bit the inside of her cheek, willing the tears to stay at bay. "Jonathan may have targeted me because he had a vendetta against my brother, but what happened to me is no one's fault but my own. I'm the one that fell for all of Jonathan's lies and didn't listen to my friends' warnings that things were moving too quickly."

"Don't be so hard on yourself. Some people are great at hiding their true character. As the old saying goes, hindsight is twenty-twenty."

"Jonathan appeared one day in the coffee shop where I worked. He soon became a regular, ordering the same drink and sitting at a corner table with a clear view of the sidewalk, the front door and the counter and work area." Kayla's mind drifted back to the first time the dark-haired, bashful man with the cute lopsided smile had worked up the nerve to speak to her. He had visited the coffee shop every day for a week. "He was older than the normal college-age crowd. When I asked if he worked nearby, he said no. That he was in his last year of grad school, working on a PhD in Behavioral Neuroscience, which seemed completely believable the way he liked to people watch."

Tears burned her eyes. Her throat tightened. She tugged her hand free, opened the protein bar and took a bite. Chewing the dry, tasteless bar, Kayla wondered how she could swallow without choking. But even choking would be better than talking about Jonathan. Heath didn't need to know how her inability to judge Jonathan's true character had made her easy prey. She'd followed him willingly into the woods where he'd planned to kill her.

# SIX

A coyote howled in the distance. Heath reached for his Glock and felt his empty holster. For a moment, he'd forgotten he'd lost his weapon. The paperwork he would have to fill out for his carelessness was going to be intense. Not to mention the ribbing his deputies were sure to give him.

Leaning back against the rock wall, he spread the hammock over his body like a blanket. The temperature behind the waterfall was colder than it had been on his previous nights on the trail. He shivered. If he wasn't afraid his movements would wake Kayla, he'd dig his extra blanket out of his pack.

"If you're cold, I'm fine sitting on the dirt floor. You can have the sleeping bag for yourself," Kayla said softly from the shadows. She'd remained silent since she'd finished eating almost an hour earlier.

"I thought you were asleep." He could barely make out her shape huddled in the corner.

"No. I can't seem to turn off my mind enough to actually sleep."

"We still have a long hike tomorrow. You need your rest."

"Yeah, well, tell that to my brain," she retorted. "Sorry. I didn't mean that the way it came out."

Every time she apologized for something she couldn't control, it pierced his conscience. He was the reason she was stuck in the woods, reliving her nightmare. And, no doubt, dealing with the post-traumatic stress associated with almost dying.

"I didn't take it negatively," he assured her. "And I don't need the sleeping bag. I have another blanket in my backpack if I get too cold. I was scooting back to stay out of the water's spray."

"Oh." There was a scraping noise, and she scurried further into the recess of the alcove, pulling her backpack and small duffel with her. "Is that better? Can you move far enough behind the wall to block the water now?"

Heath slid to his right about three feet. "I'm not crowding you, am I?"

"No. I should have—"

"Shh. I hear something." Heath strained to listen.

"Why didn't we stop at that shelter a mile back up the trail?" Larry whined.

"There's no way the sheriff can keep up his pace in the dark, not with that girl with him. I'm sure he's set up camp by now. All we've got to do is keep going until we find their campsite."

Heath stealthily pushed to his feet. Kayla followed suit, her hand clutching the back of his jacket. The men had to be close or they wouldn't be able to hear them over the roar of the waterfall. If the men looked inside the alcove, Heath and Kayla would be trapped.

"Follow me," Kayla whispered, her breath tickling his neck.

He turned toward her. "Where?"

She picked up her bags and walked backward, disappearing into the dark. He fisted the hammock and the fabric rustled.

"Shh. Listen!" Joe demanded. "What was that noise?"

"All I hear is the waterfall." A beam of light flashed on the back wall and swept toward the alcove.

"There's a cave," Joe exclaimed, followed by the sound of a rifle being cocked.

Heath dropped the hammock, picked up his backpack and moved further into the shadow. Hopefully, the light would not reach far enough inside to shine on him and Kayla huddled in the back. If Larry and Joe stepped into the alcove area, maybe Heath could throw his backpack at the men and take them by surprise.

He neared the rear wall, but Kayla was not there. Where had she gone? A hand reached out, grasped his arm and pulled him through a narrow crevice. He bumped into Kayla and she winced. He wrapped his arms around her, pulled her tight and turned sideways so he could watch the opening. *Please, Lord, don't let the killers find us.*

"There's a hammock. And a sleeping bag," Larry observed.

The flashlight beam lit up the small alcove and Heath held his breath.

"There are footprints and...what's this?" Footsteps sounded in the enclosed area. "A wrapper off of a protein bar."

"Where'd they go? And why did they leave the hammock and sleeping bag behind?"

"I don't know," Joe muttered. "But we have to be getting close to catching them."

Kayla trembled in Heath's arms and buried her face in his chest. He caressed her hair to soothe her anxiety. Although, with her ear pressed to his chest, his rapid heartbeat was sure to ramp up her nerves, countering anything he could do to ease them.

"Are you sure they aren't hiding in there somewhere?" Larry demanded.

"Look for yourself." The flashlight beam swept the back wall of the alcove. "There's no place to hide."

"Let me see." There was a scuffling of feet, as if the men were swapping places.

Heath's muscles constricted. He pulled his

arms as close to his body as he could. *Don't let them find us, Lord,* he silently pleaded. *I can't believe I have allowed myself to become trapped, with no hope of defending myself or protecting Kayla.* Her arms tightened around his waist, as if she could sense his distress over his most recent failure and wanted to provide comfort.

If Heath had originally overlooked the crevice they were hiding in, surely Larry and Joe would, too. *Please, Lord, let the men leave after a quick sweep of the light. Don't let them come far enough inside to find us.*

"Yeah, there's nothing back there. But why leave a hammock here?"

"They must have heard us coming and left in a hurry," Joe theorized. "Which means they can't be too far ahead of us. Let's go!"

Retreating footsteps echoed in their hiding place, quickly dissolving into silence.

"Tha—"

Heath placed his hand lightly over Kayla's mouth and silently counted to twenty. Pulling his hand back, he leaned in until his mouth was next to her ear. "Stay here." Then he noiselessly exited their hiding spot and crept to the opening of the alcove. A bright, white, full moon had risen and was shining through the cascading waterfall, illuminating the entire ledge area. The men were gone, and they had taken the hammock and sleeping bag with them. He quickly shifted to the other side of the waterfall and peered into the dark trail. A small light bounced over the uneven ground, moving farther and farther away.

Returning to Kayla, he found her sitting on the ground, her arms wrapped around her knees and her face hidden in her lap, the fuzzy blanket wrapped around her like a cape.

"Hey, it's okay, they're gone." He knelt beside her and touched her shoulder.

She dove into his arms and buried her face in his neck, her tears soaking his collar. "I was so scared. I kept thinking what if they hurt you and you didn't come back."

"Shh. It's okay." He stroked her head as he had earlier. "They're not going to hurt me or you. I won't let them. We *will* make it out of here."

*Stop making promises that are outside your control.* The last argument with Erin echoed in his mind. *When you're a law enforcement officer, there will be many dangerous situations you can't avoid and one of them you may not survive. If you do, but a civilian gets injured or killed, you'll carry that guilt with you the rest of your life. And it will affect you and all of your relationships.*

Kayla drew a shuddered breath, pulled back and wiped his shoulder. "I got you wet."

"It'll dry." He wanted to ask if she was okay but was afraid the question might upset her. Instead, he picked his backpack up off the ground and stepped out of the small confined space. "I know it's been a long day, but we can't stay here now. Can you hike a little further?"

"Do you think they'll come back?" She stepped out of the crevice, her pack in her hand.

"I think there's a chance they will. When they don't find us on the trail, they might circle back to look for clues." He led the way out of the alcove.

Kayla stopped and stared at the full moon. "Oh, wow. What a spectacular view of the moon. It's so bright."

"The moonlight should make it easier for us to see the trail, so we don't twist an ankle or break a leg." It could also make it easier for the killers to spot them.

"So, what's the plan?" A determined look crossed Kayla's face, the look of fear gone. "If we follow them on the trail and they decide to backtrack, they're going to see us."

"I know." Heath sighed. "We've already gone so far in this direction. If we go back the way we came, we won't make it to my truck in time to meet Sawyer tomorrow. And I'm not eager to give him additional reasons to be upset with me."

"Good point. But getting out of these woods alive is far more important than my brother's emotional state when we reach him."

Her words weren't as comforting as he suspected she'd intended them to be. Another thought struck. "If we don't show up on time,

Sawyer and my deputies are likely to form a search party to find us. And they'll start their search where we told Sawyer we would be, so we need to stick to this trail."

Kayla's brow furrowed. "Maybe if we were wearing darker colors, we'd be harder to spot."

She dropped her backpack on the ground. Then she knelt and dug inside the pack. Removing a dark long-sleeved T-shirt, she pulled it over her head. Then she stuffed the blanket into the backpack and stood. "I can't change my shoes, but hopefully, the red isn't too reflective in the moonlight."

He stood in awe of her. A few minutes ago, she was on the verge of a panic attack brought on by what he suspected was post-traumatic stress, and now she was coming up with a plan to blend in with the night.

"What do you think?" she asked, holding her arms out wide.

"I think… It could work." After shrugging out of his backpack, he located his navy-colored sweatpants and the charcoal-colored T-shirt with Parker's business logo printed on the front pocket and quickly tugged the darker clothing on over his existing outfit. Hiking in extra layers wouldn't be the most comfortable thing, but if it kept them alive overnight, it would be worth the discomfort.

* * *

Kayla's steps slowed as she stifled a yawn. Would they ever find a place to rest? Her foot connected with a tree root and she stumbled. Heath instantly grasped her elbow and prevented her from landing face-first on the trail.

"Thank you. That could have been bad." She stretched her eyes wide, desperate to force them to stay open. "I'll try to be more careful."

"You're about to fall asleep standing up."

"No, I'm—"

"Yes, you are. You've yawned twice in the last three minutes." He stopped in his tracks. "Let's set up camp."

She looked around. "We can't sleep out in the open. What if the killers return?"

"We'll go off trail. Deeper into the woods."

Kayla pressed her lips together, trapping the gasp that threatened to escape.

"I know. It's not ideal. But it's going to be okay. I promise." Heath rubbed his hand up Kayla's arm and a shiver ran along her spine. "It's your call."

Wait out in the open for the murderers to find them or venture deeper into the dark woods and hopefully find a spot to rest. What choice did she have?

"Lead the way. Before I start snoring standing up." Kayla forced a smile and prayed it covered the fear that made her quake all the way to her bones. For she knew, no matter where they found to sleep in the woods, she would not rest tonight.

"Stay close. Once we get into the trees, the moon won't light our way as much as it has on the open trail."

She nodded and stepped off the path, following him as he waded deeper into the forest. After traveling a short distance, they reached the base of a mountain. "We're not going to try to climb that in the dark, are we?" Kayla asked.

Heath took out his cell phone, turned on the flashlight and shined it around the area. He pointed at a large, gnarled oak tree. "We'll get against the mountain behind that tree. I'm not expecting rain, but it should offer some protection if the wind picks up during the night or if storm clouds move back into the region."

Kayla followed him to the tree and dropped her backpack on the ground. Thankfully, if she sat against the rock face of the mountain, no one would be able to sneak up behind her. "Are you concerned we aren't very far off the trail?"

"There's nowhere else we can go. But it should be okay. I'm a light sleeper." Heath dug into his pack and yanked out his blue poncho. "Hang on. Let me spread this on the ground so your pants won't get wet."

She settled onto it and looked up at him. "What about you?"

"I'll be fine. I can sit on my windbreaker." He

spread out his lightweight jacket and sank beside her. "I hate I let them get away with the hammock *and* the sleeping bag."

"It's not like you had a choice. We had to hide and didn't have time to gather everything. Besides, if you'd kept the hammock, the crinkling sound of the fabric would have most likely given away our hiding place."

A reflective look spanned the sheriff's face. He appeared to be a man who wasn't used to making mistakes or being caught unprepared. Sawyer had told her about several of the cases the sheriff had recently been involved in solving, including a cold case surrounding the murdered teenage daughter of a local true crime podcaster—a death the previous sheriff had written off as a suicide. Her brother had nothing but praise for the man beside her. That knowledge was the only thing keeping her emotions in check at the moment. Even though she had only known Heath for twelve hours, she had no doubt he'd do everything within his power to get her safely out of these woods.

"If Larry and Joe make it to the trailhead before us, do you think they'll give up on finding us and go on the run?" she asked hopefully.

"We've seen their faces. We know their first names. *And* we know where they buried the body. So, no. I don't. They won't want to leave behind loose ends."

An icy chill enveloped her, and she rubbed her arms.

"Are you cold?" Heath asked, concern punctuating each word. "Here, I have a down-filled top quilt I used in the hammock." He dug into his backpack.

"You keep it. I have my own." She waved him off, pulled her fuzzy multicolored blanket out of her pack, leaned back against the rock face of the mountain, draped the blanket over her body and snugged it close.

Heath shrugged and settled in beside her, dragging his backpack to rest between them. A smile sprang to her lips, but she quickly suppressed it, not wanting him to think she was laughing at his chivalrous action. He turned off the flashlight app and tucked his phone into a small side pocket. Then he retrieved the headlamp and tossed it to her. "Keep this. If something happens, and you need light, you'll have it."

*If something happens.* Her throat tightened. She closed her eyes and released a slow breath. *Lord, please don't let anything happen that separates me and Heath. I would never make it out of these woods on my own.*

Kayla placed the headlamp on her head, as it would be the only failsafe way to keep from losing it, and then she folded her arms across her stomach and closed her eyes. Hopefully, Heath would be able to get some sleep if he thought she was resting, too.

Her senses were on heightened alert, every sound of the night leaping out at her. Wind rustled through the trees. A coyote howled in the distance. A whippoorwill sang out. And Heath's breathing became slow and steady. She turned her head and peeked through her eyelashes. His chest softly rose and fell with each breath. Good. If they had any hope of making it out alive tomorrow, he needed to be rested and alert.

The moon drifted behind a cloud and panic welled up inside her as the darkness closed in. She shifted and scooted closer to Heath, her left side pressing against the backpack between them. If something happened, she could reach out and shake him awake. At least she was not alone. And she was safe—for the moment. *No, don't go there.*

She listened to Heath's breathing and tried to match hers to his. Several minutes later, as her anxiety was abating, a barn owl screeched. Kayla bolted upright and clutched Heath's arm.

"What is it?" He demanded, jumping to his feet, ready to do battle. He froze and listened. Then he turned to her. "Are you okay? What happened?"

"I'm sorry." Warmth spread up her neck. She buried her face in her hands, thankful it was too dark for him to see her humiliation and the tears that burned the backs of her eyes.

Heath scooted his backpack out of the way, sat beside her and pulled her into his arms. "Shh. Don't be sorry. Tell me what scared you."

His compassion was her undoing. The tears that had threatened flowed freely down her cheeks. The more she tried to suppress them, the harder they fell. She cried until there wasn't a single tear left and sniffles shook her body. Heath caressed her hair as he had earlier, and her sniffles subsided. She'd never known how comforting it could be to cry on the shoulder of someone who would simply hold you without trying to make things all better.

Scrubbing her hand over her face, she dried the tears off her cheeks. "Thank you."

"For what?"

*Making me feel safe.* "Being here." She met his gaze. "I am sorry I woke you."

"Don't worry about that... Can you tell me what woke you?"

"I never went to sleep." Kayla admitted.

"Do you want to talk about it?"

Did she? Not really. But after patiently holding her while she'd cried, he deserved to know what had disturbed his sleep.

"Mom and Dad instilled in me a love of the outdoors. From the time I was born, until my dad passed away when I was fifteen, we would pick a different national park each summer and spend two weeks camping and exploring. Being in the woods, surrounded by all of God's beauty, made me feel at home." She released a shuddering breath. "But that was before Jonathan took me to a cabin in the wilderness, strapped me to a chair with ten pounds of explosives, wired it to go *boom* if anyone attempted to rescue me, and left me there for three days. Alone."

"You're not alone this time. And I won't let anyone or anything hurt you." He picked up his quilt and tucked it around her.

"No. That's yours." She tried to wave it away.

"I'm fine, but you're shivering. Keep it. Please." He guided her head to his shoulder and settled back with her cradled in the crook of his arm.

She should put up more resistance and insist he take his blanket for himself, but for the first time since she'd crashed her car, she felt safe. Although, she knew the feeling wouldn't last, because soon they'd be back out on the open trail and the killers would be sure to find them.

# SEVEN

*Jonathan took me to a cabin in the wilderness, strapped me to a chair with ten pounds of explosives, wired it to go* boom *if anyone attempted to rescue me, and left me there.* Kayla's words played over and over in Heath's mind the next morning as he watched the sun rise. Being a sheriff, he knew better than most the evil that existed in this world, but there were some things that shocked even him.

Kayla had been thrown into this situation, but other than her disappointment that they had to spend the night on the trail, she hadn't complained. Not once. Even last night, when she'd been frightened and cried. Heath glanced at his companion, curled on her side with her fuzzy blanket pulled up to her neck. Her blond hair had fallen over her face, so he couldn't see her eyes. The only thing that indicated she was still asleep was the soft snore that reached his ears from time to time. They needed to get on the trail soon, but he hated to wake her.

A cool breeze blew through the canopy, rustling the leaves of the tree he sat under. He reached over and draped his blanket across her. Another thirty minutes shouldn't hurt anything.

He had only managed a couple of hours sleep, waking several times throughout the night to reassure himself that Kayla was safe and resting. She had fallen asleep quickly in his arms. Whether from sheer exhaustion from crying or because she had felt safe in his embrace, he did not know. However, each time he had woken through the night, he had been afraid to move so much as a muscle for fear of disturbing her. He'd still be laying beside her if he hadn't woken an hour earlier when his arm had fallen asleep and he'd had to wiggle free to massage it and start the blood flowing again. By the time he had gotten the feeling back in his arm, he had been wide awake and had given up on the idea of sleeping.

Heath scrubbed a hand over his face. A cup of coffee would be nice about now, but he couldn't afford to give away their location by building a fire. Puffing out a breath, he pushed to his feet and paced. The longer it took to get a crime scene team into the woods, the greater the risk of losing valuable evidence. He pulled his phone out of his pocket. No service. And only thirteen percent battery life. The rain yesterday had prevented him from using the sun to recharge the backup solar battery charger he'd been using while on the trail. Shoving his hand through his hair, he looked up and furrowed his brow.

There was a rock ledge about two-thirds of the way up the side of the mountain. If he could climb to it, would he be high enough to receive a signal? It had been several years since he'd had time to do any rock climbing. And he'd never attempted a climb without gear. Could he do it? Only one way to find out.

Heath examined the face of the mountain, mapping out a path with foot-and handholds. The morning sun lit the top of the mountain. But ten feet below the ledge, the shadows were too dark to visualize a clear path.

"What are you looking at?"

He glanced over his shoulder. "You're awake."

"Uh-huh." She stretched and pulled the head-lamp from her head. "What were you doing?"

"I was trying to decide if it would be possible to climb to that ledge."

Kayla tilted her head, a puzzled expression on her face.

"I thought I'd be able to receive cell service." Heath shook his head. "Never mind. It was a bad idea. I can't leave you. I'll just call when we get to my vehicle. A few more hours shouldn't matter as far as the crime scene. As long as the men don't move the body."

"Go." She pushed herself up to a seated position and leaned back against the mountain. "If anything happens, I have my pepper spray and you'll be close enough to hear me if I scream."

He frowned. Heath hated to leave her side for even a moment, but he was sure he could climb to the ledge in ten minutes or less. Shrugging out of his jacket, he dropped it onto the ground beside her.

The chilly morning air made the hairs on his arms stand on end. He rubbed his hands over his skin. Hopefully, he'd warm up as he started exerting himself. Even if he didn't, he couldn't afford to have his movements constricted by the outerwear. He slipped his phone into his back pocket and reached for the first handhold. *Dear Lord, please guide my way.*

Heaving out a breath, he started upward. Fifteen minutes later, his muscles quivering from exertion, he pulled himself onto the ledge and collapsed onto the cold rock surface. Sweat ran down his neck. He dragged his hand through his damp hair. That had been harder than it had looked like it would be. Heath glanced down at Kayla. She was leaned back with her head bowed. Was she praying? Or had she fallen asleep?

"Kayla. Look up," he commanded as a strong wind blew dirt and grit into his eyes. He blinked several times, fighting to focus on the woman below. She didn't budge. Was the wind preventing her from hearing him? Or had she fallen asleep? He needed to hurry so he could get back to her.

Pulling his phone out of his pocket, he looked at the screen. Three bars. A smile spread across his face. He punched in the number for the station. The phone was answered on the second ring.

"Deputy Bishop. How may I help you?"

"Bishop, it's Sheriff Dalton."

"Sheriff, are you okay? Sawyer Eldridge called and said you and his sister ran into some trouble. Men with guns are chasing y'all."

"We're fine, at the moment. Did you or Sawyer notify the rangers?"

"No, sir. We didn't have details, so we didn't know what to tell them."

He quickly told his deputy what had happened and where to locate the grave. "Since all of this has taken place inside the national park, I need you to notify the rangers' station. They'll either send out FBI agents or someone from the National Parks Service Investigative Services Branch. Ask for permission to assist."

"Yes, sir. I'll take care of everything."

"Thanks. I'll call you once Kayla and I make it back to my truck to see if you're still at the crime scene or if the coroner has taken the body to the morgue."

"Sheriff…"

"Yeah?"

"I thought you'd like to know Sawyer planned to head your way last night."

"Is the road not flooded after all the rain we've had?" Heath asked.

"Yes, but he planned to wait until midnight to head out—give the water time to recede a little. Said he'd park by your truck and hike in from there. I offered to go with him, or send another officer, but he thought it best for us to stay behind in case someone needed our assistance elsewhere."

"He was right. Besides, Sawyer is very capable. If he feels like he needs backup, I'm sure he can bring one of the Protective Instincts bodyguards with him."

Disconnecting the call, he glanced at his phone. The battery had dropped to nine percent. Another call would drain it completely. He powered it off and shoved it into his back pocket. Heath hoped Sawyer hadn't let his desire to reach his sister quickly overrule his judgment—putting his life in danger, too. Surely, the former FBI profiler had indeed brought someone with him.

"Aaaah!" Kayla's sudden, high-pitched scream sent a chill up Heath's spine.

He scrambled to the edge of the ledge and looked down. She stood staring into the woods, her blanket clutched to her chest and her back pressed against the mountain. Was there a wild animal? Or had she simply woken up and been afraid when he wasn't there? "Kayla. I'm up here."

She didn't move. Her gaze fixed on something out of his sight.

Two figures walked out of the trees, stalking their way toward her. Larry and Joe. Heath's heart sank. He had to get down the side of the mountain fast.

"Well, well, look what we have here."

"Did the sheriff abandon you?"

The voices drifted up to Heath.

"Don't come near me!" Kayla held out the pepper spray, her hand shaking.

Joe knocked the pepper spray out of her hand, and Larry snickered.

The men hadn't seen him. They didn't know he was nearby. He had to get off the mountain. *Focus. You can't save Kayla if you fall and get killed.* He gritted his teeth and pushed the chatter to the back of his mind. Then he lay on his stomach, swung his legs over the side of the ledge and eased himself down, searching for the first foothold. His foot connected with a loose rock, and it tumbled to the ground. He scrambled back onto the ledge, praying they hadn't seen him. Heath belly-crawled behind a rhododendron bush and peered between the limbs.

Three sets of eyes had turned toward the

mountain. The distance between them could not mask the fear in Kayla's eyes.

Once again, Heath's actions had caused her to be put in harm's way. Joe grabbed her as Larry raised Heath's handgun and shot in his direction, the bullet hitting the face of the mountain somewhere below where Heath hid. He held his breath, frozen in place. *Had they seen him?*

"What was that? Do you see anything?" Joe demanded.

Larry shoved the pistol into his waistband and slipped the rifle off his back. Resting the stock against his shoulder, he peered through the scope. Heath pressed his body flat against the hard rock surface of the ledge.

"No. I don't see anything," the younger man answered.

Heath desperately wanted to make his presence known—to let Kayla know he hadn't abandoned her—but doing so would be reckless.

"Where did the sheriff go?" Joe demanded.

"I don't know. I was asleep."

"He has to be close by," Larry insisted. "What kind of man would leave a woman alone in the woods?"

"Good point. Search for him. I'll hang on to our prisoner."

Kayla gasped in pain. Heath dared a look below. Joe held Kayla around the midsection, his embrace securing her arms against her sides. She struggled to get free. Deep laughter escaped the older man as he enjoyed her futile efforts.

Larry disappeared into the woods, returning several minutes later. "No sign of the sheriff anywhere."

Kayla blanched and Heath's heart squeezed. How could he have been so careless? He wanted to yell down and tell the men they'd have to fear for their lives if they dared to hurt her. But threatening men with guns would be useless and only entice them to show him who was in charge at the moment.

"I'm sure he hasn't gone far. We'll take the woman with us. That will get him to come out of hiding. Then we can shoot him," Joe declared.

"What if he doesn't catch up with us?" Larry didn't look too sure of Joe's plan.

"We use the woman as our hostage. And we get him to come to us. Somewhere out of the woods, where we have the advantage."

Kayla screamed. There was a scuffling sound. Heath leaned further over the ledge to see Joe dragging her by one arm into the woods. Headed in the direction they'd come from the night before. Away from the location where they were supposed to meet Sawyer. Kayla glanced back over her shoulder and scanned the area, her mouth dropping open as she made eye contact with him. He wanted to give her some kind of signal to let her know everything would be al-right, but she was gone before he could.

Heath exhaled a breath and swung from the ledge. He had to get off the mountain and rescue Kayla before Sawyer found them. It was going to be hard enough to explain to his friend how he'd put his younger sister in this dangerous situation in the first place, the last thing he wanted was to face Sawyer's wrath if he discovered Heath had allowed the killers to take off with her. But it wasn't only that. If something happened to the beautiful travel nurse, Heath would never be able to forgive himself.

"You're hurting me!" Kayla pulled, trying to get her arm free from her captor's grasp.

"Then stop fighting me," her abductor snarled.

*Don't allow a kidnapper to take you to a different location.* Her self-defense instructor's teachings came to mind. About ten minutes too late. Of course, she hadn't really stood much of a chance against two burly men and their guns.

*Dear Lord, I know Heath won't sit back and allow these men to take me without doing everything in his power to reach me. Please give me the wisdom to do what I need in order to slow my abductors down.*

She took a deep breath and released it slowly. *Use your soothing nurse's voice, Kayla. You have calmed many nerves through the years with your words. You can do it again.*

"Look, um…?" Not wanting to antagonize him by letting him know she knew his name, she gazed at him quizzically and waited for him to offer it.

"Joe," he snapped.

"Joe," she repeated softly. "If you'll let go of my arm, I promise I won't try to escape." He huffed in response, and she hurried on, desperate to make her point. "I'm not looking to get shot in the back. Besides, Heath and I encountered a coyote on this trail yesterday, so I will not go running through these woods alone."

He raised an eyebrow and searched her face.

"Please, I *will* follow your instructions. Because I *really* don't want to die today. Not from a gunshot and not from being mauled by a wild animal."

The younger man jerked his head in her direction. "Come on, Joe. Let her walk without you holding on to her. It's slowing us down." He narrowed his eyes. "If she tries to escape, I'll shoot her before she makes it two feet."

A cold shiver raced up her spine. She bit the inside of her lip, fighting the quiver that wanted to shake her entire body. She would not give the man the satisfaction of knowing he scared her.

After several long moments, the younger man

broke eye contact and turned away. "Let her arm go, Joe. Then you take the lead and…"

"Kayla." The metallic taste of blood slid down her throat. She coughed. She'd bitten her lip too hard.

"Kayla can walk between us. That way, I can keep an eye on her and make sure she doesn't try anything." Larry smirked.

Her stomach lurched and bile rose in her throat. His smile reminded her of the one Jonathan had given her right after he'd forcibly kissed her seconds before he'd walked out of the cabin, leaving her to die. On that day, she'd promised herself, if she got out of there alive, she'd never allow herself to be put in a situation where someone could murder her in the wilderness and her body never be found.

"Okay, Larry, but don't let her get away." Joe released his hold on her arm.

Kayla pressed her lips together and turned away from Larry. *Do not give them the satisfaction of seeing your fear. Do as they say so they don't tie you up. Or shoot you. No, they won't shoot you. Not until they kill Heath and escape his deputies.*

She concentrated on putting one foot in front of the other, not allowing herself to think about what they would do to her once they didn't need her any longer. Right now, the focus had to be on following instructions so they didn't bind her hands.

"Good girl." Larry laughed. "Guess you know who's in charge here."

Joe swung around, and Kayla stopped short to keep from running into him. The older man shoved her to the right and stomped past her. "You're not in charge of anything. I'm the oldest. I don't answer to you."

"You're the reason we're in this mess. If you would have listened to me and tossed Ray's body in Fontana Lake, we wouldn't be in this situation."

"And if you hadn't let Ray find out about our *little* drug business, I wouldn't have had to kill him in the first place." Joe rose to his full height and put his face inches from Larry's.

Kayla looked around. Could she run away while they were distracted? She slowly inched backward, toward a grove of pine trees bordering the trail.

"You need to learn to keep your mouth shut." Larry shoved Joe's chest. "You don't need to talk about those things in front of our prisoner."

Joe scoffed. "It's not like she's going to tell anyone. You and I both know she'll be dead before nightfall."

Kayla's back made contact with a tree. She turned and ran. A gunshot rang out, a bullet hitting a tree a few feet in front of her and to her right.

"Stop right there!" Larry commanded.

She froze, raised both hands and turned to face the men, her body trembling. How could she have been so foolish? Larry advanced in her direction. The rifle trained on her. *Lord, please, don't let him shoot me.*

Larry gripped her upper arm and pulled her back to the trail. "I thought you agreed to follow instructions. Do you want me to shoot you right here and leave your body for the wild animals to eat?"

"N-no," she stammered, shaking her head.

"Guess I can't blame you for trying to escape, since my cousin was distracting my attention. But…" He shoved the rifle barrel in her side. "Don't try it again. Because I won't give you another chance. Got it?"

Kayla closed her eyes and nodded.

They reached the spot where Joe waited. Larry shoved her in his direction. "Use your belt or something to tie her to you."

"No," she pleaded. "I promise. I'll behave."

Larry bent down, his face inches from hers. "If you don't, I'll put a bullet through your head," he said. His breath smelled like rancid onions, and her eyes watered.

"Do you hear me?" he demanded.

She pressed her lips together and nodded. As

soon as he stepped back, she released her breath and inhaled a deep gulp of fresh air. Larry glared at her with a raised eyebrow. Then he turned back to the trail.

"Do what he says. You don't want to cross him," Joe muttered under his breath.

"And you." Larry motioned to Joe. "Stop gabbing and get moving. We need to put as much distance between us and that sheriff as we can. You know he ain't smart enough to hang back. If we don't get out of here before he catches up with us, there will be a shoot-out. You're the one who keeps putting us in situations to get us caught. So, I promise you, if things go wrong, I won't be worried about anyone but myself."

"If you'd give me one of the weapons—"

"That ain't happening. I've seen your aim before. You will not get a chance to shoot me." Larry straightened the strap of the rifle that was slung over his shoulder, then he waved the gun, motioning they should get moving.

Joe turned and started along the trail, shooting glances backward over his shoulder.

Was the older man afraid of the younger one? From a distance, it had seemed Joe was the one in charge, but now that Kayla was up close, listening to them interact, she wasn't so sure. The only thing she was sure of was she needed to follow Larry's commands while she stayed focused and looked for an opportunity to escape. If it wasn't for the heavy rains and floods in the area, she had no doubt Sawyer would have already made it to her, but he hadn't. Heath would reach her first, but he didn't have a weapon. It would be up to her to save herself. If she could get a grip on her emotions and not let her fear control her. *Lord, help me!*

# EIGHT

Heath dug his fingernails into the side of the mountain. Pain radiated through his shoulders and his arms shook. Getting down was taking twice as long as it had taken him to climb up. He had not calculated how difficult it would be to descend without gear. One wrong move and he would be dead. That wouldn't help Kayla. If she were still alive. No. Heath could not let his mind go there. The gunshot he'd heard could have been a hunter. *It's not hunting season.* It could have been a warning shot to scare off a wild animal. Whatever had triggered the gunshot, he had to get off the mountain and reach Kayla.

Glancing under his arm, he tried to gauge the distance to the ground. Was he close enough to let go and drop without breaking a leg?

*Lord, let this work and let me reach Kayla before they harm her.*

He exhaled, planted his feet against the rock face and swung out as he would if he were repelling. Then he let go his grip, dropped to the ground and rolled. The wind was knocked out of him. He lay there for several long seconds, taking deep breaths.

The sound of someone or something moving through the woods reached him. He sprang to his feet, looking for a weapon. Picking up a large rock the size of a softball, he scooted behind the tree they had slept behind the night before. And waited.

Two men stepped into the clearing. Heath released a sigh of relief. Sawyer. And Parker. He hadn't expected to see his brother, but he was thrilled reinforcements had arrived.

"I'm so glad you're here." He rushed over to them.

"You'd better be," Parker joked, giving him a one-armed hug. "Hiking through the woods in the middle of the night isn't my idea of fun. I would—"

"Where's Kayla?" Sawyer asked, looking around the area.

Heath met Kayla's brother's gaze. "The killers have her."

"What!"

"They passed us last night on the trail. We didn't catch up to them, so I was confident we were safe here." He sighed. "But I was wrong."

"You put my sister's life in danger," Sawyer raged, "and then you let the killers take her?"

"Hey, I know you're worried about your sister." Parker put a hand on Sawyer's shoulder defensively. "But my brother would never purposefully put anyone in harm's way. Give him a chance to tell us what happened."

"I'll tell you on the way." Heath noted the rifle slung across his brother's back. "Is that the only weapon y'all brought?"

"Of course not." Sawyer pulled back his jacket to reveal a shoulder holster. "Didn't you bring a weapon on your camping trip?"

The question he'd dreaded most. Heath clenched his teeth and met his friend's eyes. "I did. The killers have it." He did an about-face and headed in the direction Larry and Joe had taken Kayla. "Let's go. They have a thirty-minute head start."

The two men fell into place behind him on the narrow trail, following his lead without question. As they walked, the silence stretched out until it became almost deafening. "There are two men. Larry and Joe. Don't know last names. I found them burying a body." Heath took a deep breath and released it slowly. "I tried to apprehend them, but they got the jump on me. And I got shot."

"They shot you? Where? Are you hurt?" Parker rushed up beside him and caught his arm, halting his steps.

"I'm fine. The bullet grazed my shoulder.

Kayla dressed the wound last night." Heath jerked free of his brother's grasp and turned to Sawyer. "I really am sorry that I put your sister in this situation. I never would have stepped out into the road in front of her vehicle if I had known this would happen."

"I know. I'm sorry I—" Sawyer swallowed his words and shoved a hand through his hair. "Tell me how Kayla ended up being taken."

"Larry and Joe passed us last night. We were hiding behind the waterfall. We decided—I decided—we needed to move our campsite in case they came back. It was either follow behind them or turn back in the opposite direction. I made the call for us to trail them, since they obviously thought that we were still ahead of them. And it would put us closer to the place we planned to meet you."

"You said they took her this morning. That means you didn't catch up to them last night," Sawyer surmised.

"No. Last night, after hiking for a couple of hours, we went off trail and camped where you found me." Heath's steps slowed. "How did y'all find me?"

"We heard a noise, so we checked it out." Parker shrugged. "You weren't that far off the trail."

If he hadn't dropped the last few feet off the

side of the mountain, would they have walked right on by without knowing he was there? Wait. Was that how Larry and Joe had found them earlier? Had the men heard him on the phone and followed the sound of his voice? *Lord, how could I have been so careless?*

Resolve washed over him. It was time he took control of this situation once and for all. He would find Kayla and get her to safety, and he would capture Larry and Joe.

"Let's pick up the pace." Heath took off along the trail again, this time at a near jog. Sawyer kept pace with him, Parker following close behind.

"You didn't tell me how they kidnapped my sister."

"I thought we were in a safe location, so I climbed partway up the mountain to get cell service to call the station. I had finished the call and was about to head back down, when Larry and Joe showed up. When I attempted to reach Kayla, they shot in my direction. I—" He pressed his lips together and shook his head.

"It's okay." Sawyer clapped him on the shoulder. "I know you would have stopped them if you could have. We *will* get her back."

An hour and a half later, they reached the waterfall. There was no sign of Kayla or the men. Heath did a quick search of the alcove area behind the waterfall. "I really thought we would have caught up to them by now."

"Let's think positively. We've not found any signs of a scuffle. No blood or bod—" Parker bit off his words when Heath glared at him.

"While I wouldn't have worded it quite that way, I agree with Parker's sentiment. Unless we come across evidence to the contrary, we will continue to believe Kayla is alive and well." Sawyer cleared his throat. "My sister's a fighter. She didn't survive a serial killer to die in these woods at the hands of two random men."

"Agreed. Your sister is one of the bravest women I've ever met. She'll do whatever it takes to stay alive. And she knows I won't give up until she's safe." Heat crept up Heath's neck as he endured Sawyer's gaze. Was the former profiler reading more into Heath's words than he'd intended? "I promised Kayla I'd get her out of these woods alive. I'm a man of my word."

*And the sheriff.* It was his responsibility to protect the citizens in his county. Sure, that's all it was. His need to rescue her from the killers had nothing to do with the way his breath caught when Kayla looked at him.

*Lord, please don't let me break my promise to Kayla. I dreaded facing Sawyer and telling him she'd been abducted, but if anything happens to her, it will be my own image in the mirror that I won't be able to face.*

\* \* \*

If she had thought yesterday's hike through the wilderness had been scary and exhausting, Kayla now knew better. It had been a breeze compared to the past four hours. Her calves throbbed and the soles of her feet burned. The friction from her shoes had caused one of the bandages she'd put over her blisters yesterday to come loose and now it was a lumpy, sticky blob under her heel.

"You can move faster than that," Larry declared. He had pushed her and Joe to move at a dangerous pace through the narrowest parts of the trail as he'd muttered about the need to stay ahead of the sheriff.

She'd had enough. Angering Larry could get her shot; however, if they continued to race recklessly along the trail, it was likely that she would end up at the bottom of the ravine with a broken neck. Either way, she'd be dead. She spun around to face the man who had been walking behind her to *keep her in line*. "Moving faster is dangerous."

"Yeah. So is not moving faster." He lifted the gun and pointed it at her head.

"Fine. Shoot me. Get it over with." Kayla folded her arms over her chest.

Larry's face reddened. "You think I won't?"

"Actually, I know you will. As soon as you decide you don't need me anymore. I'm not naïve."

"Who says I need you past this point where we are now?"

She pressed her lips together and waited. Her heart was in her throat. *Dear Lord, if today is my last day on earth, please make my passing quick.*

"Stop it!" Joe demanded. "Larry, you know you won't shoot her."

"Are you sure about that?"

"You'd never *get your hands dirty.* You leave all that stuff up to me. And I say we need her to be our hostage if we hope to make it out of these woods alive."

The men glared at each other as if they were engaged in a silent battle of wills. Several long minutes passed with Kayla trapped between them, afraid to speak or move a muscle.

"Fine," Larry said through gritted teeth. "We'll slow our pace going down this sloped area. But only until we reach the bottom."

There was a flash of light on the ridge above them. The sun had glinted off something. Could it be Heath? Had he caught up to them? Kayla fisted her hands and resisted the urge to shade her eyes. As desperate as she was to figure out if the glint of light was simply her imagination playing tricks on her, she couldn't risk alerting her abductors. In case it was Heath coming to her rescue.

The object glinted once more. Someone was

definitely making their way across the ridge toward them.

Joe pointed in the distance. "Hey, Larry, look at—"

"Thank you," she interrupted, hoping to distract the men from what she suspected Joe had seen.

Two sets of eyes turned toward her.

"For agreeing to slow the pace." She swallowed. The words had tasted like vinegar.

"I'm not doing it for you." The younger man frowned. "Like Joe said, the only way we can get out of here alive is if we have you as a hostage." He turned to Joe. "What did you want me to see?"

The older man shook his head. "I don't see it now. Guess it was nothing."

"Okay, let's go." Larry motioned with the rifle for them to move along the path.

*Lord, I pray it is Heath behind us. Please let him save me.*

If Kayla was correct and the movement she'd seen was Heath, she estimated he was about five minutes behind them. Once they reached the flatter ground at the bottom of the incline, her abductors would force her to move faster. It was up to her to do what she could to give the sheriff a chance to catch up with them. She slowed her pace as much as she dared, randomly using the side of her foot to send a loose rock tumbling down the mountain to reinforce the idea that the path was treacherous.

"You can go faster than that," Larry barked.

Kayla spun around to glare at him, lost her footing and slid down. She tried to break her fall. Rocks and gravel bit into her hands, burning and stinging. Tears welled in her eyes, and she blinked them away. If she wanted to stay alive long enough for Heath to reach her, she couldn't afford to show any weakness.

"Get up!" Larry grabbed her by the shirt collar and pulled her to her feet. He scowled, baring his teeth. "I know what you're doing. But it won't work."

Only one way to deal with a bully. Face him head-on. "What exactly is it you *think* I'm doing? You're the one that yelled, startling me and causing me to fall."

"You're stalling. Because you think the sheriff will rescue you. He won't. If he tracks us, I'll shoot him before he gets too close." Larry sneered and waved the pistol in her face. "He couldn't even hold on to his gun. Without a weapon, he doesn't stand a chance of capturing us. Or saving you."

He turned her around and shoved her between the shoulder blades. "Now, get going. And don't pull any more stunts."

Joe had stopped to watch the interaction. She met his gaze. The look in his eyes was one of pure hate. Only, she couldn't tell if his anger was directed at her or at Larry. These men were a puzzle. Of course, anyone who would take another human life was someone she would never understand.

Continuing to make her way along the rocky path, she tried to formulate a plan. When Jonathan had abducted her, she'd been too frightened to fight for her life. She'd withdrawn into a shell and had accepted that her life was about to end. Then Sawyer had showed up. And she had been afraid her brother was going to die, too, and it would be her fault.

Her mind spun like a ride at an amusement park. What Larry had said about Heath not having a gun played on repeat in her brain. Having spent the better part of the past twenty-four hours with the sheriff, she knew he wouldn't give up and would do his best to save her. She couldn't allow him to risk his life for her, even if putting his life on the line was part of his job. Sawyer would have a gun but they weren't supposed to meet him for several hours.

Though, knowing her big brother, it wouldn't surprise her if he was already in the woods hiking to meet them. Only, they wouldn't meet up along the trail, not with her being abducted and Heath trailing her. Sawyer must be frantic, wondering where she and Heath were. She had to get away from these men.

Reducing her pace, she glanced over her shoulder. If she could get Larry to talking, maybe she could distract him and escape. "I think I misjudged you. When I saw you two yesterday, I thought Joe was the one in charge."

The younger man scoffed. "As if."

"Actually." She shrugged. "Hea—Sheriff Dalton seemed to have the same impression."

"Well, you're both wrong." He came even with her. "Joe's too dumb to be in charge."

"Hey! I'm not dumb. When I see a problem, I fix it." Joe huffed.

"You fixed it alright. If you had let me handle things, I would have made it look like Ray's death was an accident."

The older man stopped short, turned and pulled to his full height. "I told you. I had a plan to make it look like a suicide. There was a note and everything, written in Ray's own handwriting."

"Yeah. Well, I think you'd have a hard time making the medical examiner believe a man shot himself while tied to a chair."

"I was going to untie him after I shot him. Only, you came back too soon."

"And how were you going to explain the rope burns on his wrists and ankles?"

"It would have been days before anyone found his body. The rope burns would have disappeared by then."

"And that's why I called you dumb." Larry

clenched his jaw. One of the veins in his neck bulged. "After a person is dead, the body does not heal. Contusions don't just *disappear.*"

"Yeah, when did you get your medical degree?" Red splotches crept up Joe's neck. "You wouldn't even wait to see what happened, insisting we dispose of the body immediately."

"If we had waited until his body started to decompose, the entire shop would have smelled like rotting flesh." Larry turned his back on Kayla so he could glare at his cousin. "And if you wouldn't have insisted on burying the body in the woods, we wouldn't have spent the night traipsing through the wilderness after a sheriff who can identify us."

"You are the one who let Ray find out about the drugs. Besides, if we'd dumped him in the lake, it would have only been a matter of time before his body floated to the surface. Burying him in a remote area was our only hope of his body not being discovered. And if you hadn't grumbled and complained so much, we could have had the grave dug a lot sooner and been out of there before the sheriff stumbled upon us." Joe fisted his hands, anger radiating from him. "I'm always the one cleaning up your messes."

"Oh, yeah." Larry stepped closer, his face inches from Joe's.

Kayla looked around. She searched the horizon, looking for a sign that Heath was nearby. Nothing. She was on her own.

"Get outta my face!" Joe shoved Larry. He stumbled into her. The pistol in his waistband jabbed her in the side.

Before she could think through her actions, she wrapped her hand around the handle, pulled the weapon free, stepped to the side and pointed the gun at the men. She didn't want to kill anyone, but she would if it was the only way to get out of these woods alive.

# NINE

"Don't move!" Kayla's voice rang out from nearby.

Heath raced in the direction the sound had come from, Sawyer and Parker at his heels. They topped the ridge and his breath caught. Kayla was fifty yards away—halfway down the side of the mountain—with a gun in her hand, pointed at her abductors.

Joe stood like a statue with his hands in the air. But Larry advanced toward Kayla while reaching for his rifle.

"Kayla's blocking my shot. If I get a clear view, do you want me to take him out?" Parker asked as he leaned his elbows on a boulder and braced his gun against his shoulder.

"I'd prefer to take him alive, if possible." Heath spared a quick glance in his brother's direction. "But if you have to shoot, make sure Kayla isn't in the line of fire."

"Of course."

A former marine, his brother was a trained

sniper. Heath trusted him with a weapon more than any other person he knew, but he couldn't just sit there and watch everything play out. There had to be a way for him to get closer without being seen.

Bordering the trail on the left side was a steep drop-off, but the right side butted against a mountain wall with a scattering of trees and large boulders every few feet. "I'm going to move closer."

"*We* are moving closer," Sawyer said, his tone leaving no room for argument. "These guys don't know me. I'll pretend to be a hiker who just stumbles upon them."

Not taking his eyes off the scene playing out below, Heath nodded his agreement. Sawyer was a trained agent. He knew the risks. Besides there'd be no talking him out of it if he'd made up his mind.

Larry had his rifle trained on Kayla, but she wasn't backing down, her weapon pointed at the killer's chest.

"Does she know how to shoot?" Heath asked.

"Yes. But only at paper targets. We need to get down there fast."

Heath held out his hand. "Give me your weapon."

Sawyer hesitated for a split second before he pulled it out of his shoulder holster and gave it to him. "I need your backpack."

Heath tucked the pistol into his waistband then shrugged off his pack and handed it over.

"Go. I've got you covered," Parker said, his focus never wavering as he looked through the scope on his rifle.

Heath darted to the first tree then quickly dashed from one hiding place to the next until he was halfway to Kayla. Physically and emotionally, his progress felt like it was taking hours, but logically he knew it couldn't have been more than a couple of minutes. At the moment, Kayla and Larry appeared to be in a standoff.

He motioned for Sawyer to start down the mountain and watched as he stealthily made his way along the trail. *Please, Lord, don't let Larry shoot anyone. I pray we take the men into custody without incident.*

"Put down the gun," Larry commanded, a slight quiver in his voice giving away his uncertainty. "You don't have what it takes to shoot me. And I'm done playing games with you."

"Don't test me," Kayla replied, her voice steady and confident, leaving little doubt she meant what she said. "I have excellent aim."

Sawyer made eye contact with Heath. He palmed his weapon and nodded. Then the former profiler took several heavy footsteps. Three sets of eyes turned in his direction. Sawyer skidded to a halt twenty feet from the trio. "Sorry. Almost didn't see y'all there. Guess I was focused on staying upright on this steep incline."

Kayla's jaw dropped but, to her credit, she quickly snapped it closed and turned her attention back to the killers. Joe inched backward a few steps, looking over his shoulder as if searching for an escape. While Larry stood his ground, his rifle rotating between Kayla and Sawyer.

"Who are you?" Larry demanded. "What are you doing here?"

"What does it look like I'm doing here? I'm hiking." Sawyer's eyes widened as if he'd just noticed the guns. "Whoa. Whatever this is…" He pointed his finger from Larry to Kayla and back again. "Doesn't concern me. I'll just be on my way."

Sawyer took a step as if to go around the group, but Larry blocked his path, the gun firmly trained on him. "You're not going anywhere."

"No, but you are." Heath stepped out from his hiding place with his weapon trained on the killer.

A smile split Kayla's face when she saw him. Heath's heart warmed. Once he got his prisoners locked in a jail cell, he needed to find a way to make up for all he'd put her through.

"Put your weapon down, Larry. It's over." Heath jerked his head toward the top of the trail.

Shock registered on Larry's face when he spotted Parker leaning against the boulder, his rifle pointed at him. He took two steps back, precariously close to the edge of the mountain. His eyes darted from Parker to Heath and Kayla. Both still had their weapons aimed at him.

"Don't do it," Sawyer said softly. "You might get one round off, but the instant you do, whomever you didn't shoot will drop you."

Larry eyed Kayla.

"I know what you're thinking. Shoot the sheriff first then get off as many rounds as possible."

"Is that so?"

"It is logical. The man on the ridge is far away. Surely, his shot would miss. And the woman, although she's standing closer, is probably not a very good marksman." Sawyer continued, "Do you want me to tell you what's wrong with your train of thought?"

"Who are you?" Larry demanded.

"Someone who doesn't want to get caught in the middle of a shoot-out."

Larry turned his gun on Sawyer. Kayla gasped. Heath took a step in her direction, and Larry's weapon swung back to him again. "Okay, tell me why I shouldn't take my shot at the sheriff here."

"You don't know what kind of weapon the guy on the ridge has. I do. I also know he's a trained military sniper. The only reason you're still standing is because the sheriff wants you alive," Sawyer replied matter-of-factly. "As for the woman. She may not be a trained sniper, but she can drop you just as quickly. I should know. I'm the one who taught her how to shoot—the last time someone kidnapped her and tried to kill her."

"Is that so?" Uncertainty punctuated Larry's words.

Sawyer nodded.

"I guess I don't have a choice then." Larry spread his arms wide and opened his hands. His gun dropped over the side of the mountain.

Joe, who'd been quietly hiding in the background, suddenly turned and ran, racing for the bottom of the mountain. Heath jerked his head toward the fleeing felon. "Sawyer, stop him."

Without a second's hesitation, Sawyer unsnapped the pack he'd been wearing, dropped it on the ground and darted after the fleeing man.

Heath kept his attention focused on Larry. "Kayla, grab the rope from my backpack."

Walking sideways, her weapon never wavering, Kayla made her way to the pack and retrieved the rope.

"Okay, Larry put your hands on your head, take one step forward and turn around." To Heath's amazement, the man did as commanded without comment. Heath glanced over his shoulder. Good. Parker was still in position.

Heath accepted the rope from Kayla. Then he tucked his weapon into the back of his waistband and stepped up to his prisoner.

"This isn't over," Larry declared. Then he did a dive roll over the side of the mountain.

Drawing his weapon, Heath dashed to the edge. Larry tumbled over the uneven ground, bouncing all the way to the bottom, and landed in a thicket of mountain laurel.

Kayla rushed to Heath's side. "Where is he?"

"He landed in those shrubs, but I don't see him now." He searched the landscape below.

Footsteps sounded behind them. Parker sprinted toward them. "Did we lose him? I couldn't get a clear shot. You were between me and him."

"It's okay." Heath tied the end of the rope to a medium-sized tree. The rope was shorter than he'd like, but it would help him bypass some bumps Larry had suffered on his route to the bottom. "He got pretty banged up on his way down. I should be able to pick up his trail once I get there."

"I'm going with you." Parker slipped his rifle strap over his head and reached for the rope.

"No. I need you to get Kayla out of these woods."

"You can't go alone." Kayla grabbed his arm. "He's dangerous."

"It's my job to chase and capture the bad guys." Heath reached up and caressed her cheek. "To keep people safe. But the only way I can do my job is if Parker takes you out of here. Because, right now, your safety is most important to me."

A lone tear slipped down her cheek, and he brushed it away with his thumb. Then he pulled her into a tight hug. Looking over her shoulder, he saw Sawyer approaching—a firm grasp on Joe's arm. *Thank you, Lord.* One of the killers had been captured. The profiler lifted an eyebrow and tilted his head. What was going through his mind? No time to worry about Kayla's brother and what he thought the hug might mean. It was time for Heath to capture the other killer.

He pulled back and turned to Parker, who stood staring at him with an odd expression on his face. "Don't let anything happen to her."

Kayla held out his gun. "I believe this is yours."

"Thanks. You take this one." Heath gave her Sawyer's Glock. "It's your brother's."

"I'll take that," Sawyer announced, jogging up to them, half dragging Joe behind him. "So, what's the plan? I saw the other guy do a not-so-graceful dive off the side of the mountain as I tackled this one." He held out his hand and Kayla placed the gun in his palm.

"The plan is that I'm going to go after Larry. You and Parker will get Kayla out of here and turn Joe here over to one of my deputies."

"Parker, can you watch this guy? I need a word with the sheriff." Sawyer waved his gun at a shaded area and motioned for Joe to sit down.

Parker and Kayla moved to stand near the prisoner while Sawyer pulled Heath aside.

"I understand you want to chase after that guy and capture him, but do you really think you're in any shape to do so?"

"What do you mean? Of course, I—"

"You've just completed a week-long hiking trip and, for the last twenty-four hours, you've been on high alert, avoiding killers and keeping my sister alive. I'm just wondering how much sleep you got last night, and if you're truly up to chasing after this guy."

"Look. I can't let him get away."

"I'm just saying you're not thinking clearly right now."

"How so?"

"You hugged my sister. A woman you've known roughly twenty-four hours."

"And?"

"I've known you for three years, Heath. You're always professional. The only person I've seen you hug is your mother."

"It meant nothing. Your sister has been through a traumatic experience because of my carelessness. I was comforting her. That's all."

"I appreciate that. Now, I'm going to do something for you." Sawyer tugged the rope out of Heath's hands. "Get my sister out of here." He pushed off and dropped over the edge of the mountain.

Kayla and Parker rushed up to Heath.

"Where's he going?" Kayla demanded.

"After Larry. It seems he's forgotten who's the sheriff." Heath met her eyes. "Don't worry. I'm following him."

He glanced at Joe, who was seated on the ground with his hands and feet tied together. Then he turned to Parker. "Can you take him and turn him over to my deputies? They should be at the gravesite. It's about two miles from the entrance of the trail Dad always took us on for hikes when we were kids. Kayla can show you where once you get close." Heath looked at her to confirm and she nodded.

"Don't worry about us," Parker said.

"Be careful," Kayla ordered, concern written all over her face.

He nodded, grasped the rope and repelled off the side of the mountain. Time to catch a killer.

Three hours later, Heath and Sawyer stepped out of the forest and onto the side of a road.

"Looks like we lost him." Heath clenched his jaw and shook his head.

They had trailed the killer through thick woods and had even exchanged gunfire at one point, but he'd still managed to give them the slip. A truck came into view, sped up as it neared them and zoomed past. Heath couldn't blame the driver.

After a week on the trail, he was sure he looked rough.

"He probably hitched a ride with someone. Let's pray he doesn't repay their kindness with a bullet to their head." Sawyer looked around. "Do you recognize this road?"

"No, but I'm sure we're still in the national park." He pointed to the right. "If my sense of direction is correct—which it may not be considering all the twists and turns we've taken—we need to go this way."

"Since I have no clue where we are, I'll follow your lead." Sawyer fell into step beside him. Then he pulled out his cell phone. "No service. I'll check when we get to the top of this hill. You would pick the direction that requires us to go uphill."

Heath chuckled at his friend's teasing. "Sorry about that." He wiped sweat off his forehead. "I pray Kayla and Parker have made it to safety. And that Joe has been taken into custody."

"I'm sure they have. Your brother strikes me as a very responsible person."

"He is. Since he left the military, it's taken him a while to figure out the direction he wants his life to take. I think he's on the right path with his new business, but only time will tell."

"It's not uncommon for people who have left the military to take a few years to figure out what they want to do next. He seems to have a good head on his shoulders."

"Thanks. I'm proud of him." Heath turned at the sound of a vehicle coming behind them. "It's a park ranger." He waved his arm. *Please stop.*

The ranger turned on the roof-bar lights, pulled up beside them and rolled a window down partway. "Hitchhiking in a national park is a federal offense."

Heath pulled his ID and held it out. "We aren't hitchhikers. I'm Sheriff Heath Dalton and this is Sawyer Eldridge. We—"

"Sheriff Dalton, I'm Ranger Meghan Harris. I know some people who will be happy to see you both." She unlocked the doors. "Hop in."

"We're following a killer. We think he may have caught a ride in this area," Heath said as he climbed into the front seat.

"He's long gone if he did. This road leads out of the park. The exit is just over the hill." She made a U-turn and headed in the opposite direction. "I'll take you to headquarters. Agent Knight is heading up the investigation. He will have questions for you. Plus, that's where your brother and Mr. Eldridge's sister are waiting."

Sawyer leaned forward. "Is Kayla okay? Has a paramedic checked her out?"

"Yes, sir. She was also given something to eat and a drink with electrolytes."

"You seem to know everything that's going on, Ranger Harris," Heath observed.

"I'm the one who drove Kayla and Parker to the medical clinic and then to headquarters for questioning." She glanced at him. "I'd just left there when I was asked to check out a report of a hitchhiker in the park. It was probably your guy."

Ranger Harris activated her blinker and turned into ranger headquarters, parking in a spot close to the entrance.

Heath opened his door. "Thank you, for taking care of Kayla and for giving us a lift."

"My pleasure. From all I've heard, you've been through an ordeal the past two days." She exited the vehicle. "I'll show you the way."

She led them into the building and guided them to a small conference room, where Kayla and Parker waited.

"Oh, thank God, you're alive!" Kayla jumped up and raced toward them, barreling into Heath's arms.

He returned her embrace, refusing to analyze why she'd hugged him and not Sawyer. Gratefulness washed over him. She was safe. Now, he only had to track down Larry and put him in jail so he could never harm her again.

# TEN

"I really would be okay at the cabin. All I'm going to do is take a bath and go straight to bed." Kayla knew she was wasting her breath. She also knew that her brother loved her. And it wouldn't hurt her to spend one night at his house to give him peace of mind, but tomorrow she would get a rental car and check into the cabin she'd rented.

Sawyer slowed his speed, activated his blinker and turned onto the gravel drive that led to his house. "You really want me to face Bridget and tell her I left you alone, with a killer still on the loose?"

An image of Kayla's petite, redheaded sister-in-law popped into her mind. "Are you afraid of your wife?"

"No...but she loves you. And she would be worried about you. I would, too. You know that." He pulled to a stop in front of his two-story farmhouse, put the vehicle into Park and turned to face her. "If you really want to be alone, I'll turn around now and take you to the cabin."

She searched her big brother's face. The tired expression and shadows under his eyes made him appear much older than the twelve years that separated them. Kayla felt like a spoiled brat. Sawyer had rescued her from a killer—not once, but twice. It would not hurt her to spend one night in his home so he'd rest, knowing she was safe.

"With so many officers searching for him, Larry may have already been captured. Even if he hasn't, the odds of him finding me are very slim. He doesn't know my full name or where I'm staying."

Sawyer's expression remained blank. She sighed and reached for the door handle. "Okay. I'll stay. *One* night. It's not like I would pass up a chance for baby snuggles, no matter how tired I am."

Sawyer bound out of the driver's seat, jogged around the vehicle and retrieved her bag from the back. "Good, I—"

"*One night*," she reemphasized. "Tomorrow I will need to arrange for a rental car, have my vehicle towed and—"

"I forgot to tell you. I called Amos Cline last night and arranged for him to tow your car to his shop. He was supposed to drop your luggage off here."

Why was Kayla not surprised? She knew he hadn't meant anything by his actions. His assumption that she'd come stay with them now was just part of who he was. Maybe because their dad had left his mom when Sawyer was young, and he had spent his childhood believing he had to be the man of the house—that it was up to him to ensure the happiness and safety of the women he loved.

She looped her arm through his as they walked up the walkway. "Thank you."

The front door burst open, and Bridget stepped onto the porch, eighteen-month-old Vincent perched on her hip. "Oh, I'm so glad you're here. I've been so worried about you." She gave Sawyer a quick kiss, passed Vincent to him and swooped Kayla into a big hug. "Are you okay?"

Kayla returned her sister-in-law's hug. "I'm fine. Just tired. And I could use a hot shower."

"Of course." Bridget drew back and led the way into the house. "I put your luggage in the guest room. Go on up, get a shower and change clothes. I have a roast in the oven. Dinner will be on the table when you come back down."

"That sounds good. Thank you." Kayla leaned over and kissed Vincent's cheek. He giggled and buried his face in his dad's shoulder. She tussled his strawberry-blond hair, turned and headed up the stairs. "I'll be quick. Maybe fifteen minutes."

"Take as much time as you need," Sawyer called after her.

Kayla looked over her shoulder and watched as her brother crossed to the playpen in the corner of the living room and placed Vincent inside it, then turned, grasped Bridget's hand and led her to an oversized leather chair. The couple sat, snuggled up, whispering. Sawyer was probably catching Bridget up on all that had transpired.

A pang stabbed Kayla's heart. She had always hoped for a relationship like the one her parents had—that her brother and sister-in-law now had. Sadly, that was not something that would be in her future. Since Jonathan's betrayal and his attempt on her life, the thought of dating, becoming engaged and marrying paralyzed her.

The past four years had taught her to be okay being alone. Actually, she really liked her own company and didn't feel the need to be around others as it was uncomfortable answering all the questions about what she'd gone through. *Until Heath.* Why hadn't it been awkward to talk to him about Jonathan? Because he was a sheriff, not a friend or family member. *Sure. Tell yourself that.* She jogged up the remaining few steps.

Entering the guest room, she went to her luggage, sat on the floor, dug out her phone charger and plugged it into the nearest outlet. Her phone battery was dead. Her mother was probably worried sick about her, especially since Kayla hadn't messaged to let her know she'd made it safely to Barton Creek. However, it wasn't her mother that she was most eager to hear from, but the sheriff of Blount County.

After she and Sawyer had given their statements, she'd looked for Heath but he had been in an office with FBI agents, mapping out a plan to track and capture Larry.

*Please, Lord, let Sawyer hear from Heath soon. I pray they've captured Larry and that Heath is safe.*

With a sigh, she grabbed a change of clothes and headed to the bathroom.

Fifteen minutes later, she finished drying her hair and gathered it into a ponytail. Time to join the family for dinner and face all of Bridget's questions, which she was sure her inquisitive sister-in-law would have plenty of. Reentering the bedroom, she glanced at her phone. Eleven text messages. Eight of those, and two missed phone calls, were from her mother.

Biting her lip, she weighed her options. Call Mom and explain why she'd been MIA for the past thirty hours or wait and call her tomorrow, increasing her mother's anxiety. Taking a deep breath and releasing it slowly, she quickly typed a message to her mom.

Sorry I haven't called. Cell service has been spotty. Having dinner with Sawyer and Bridget. Will call you tomorrow. Love you!

Kayla hated to worry her mother, but she wasn't ready to tell Mom about her recent ordeal. And she'd never been good at keeping se-crets from her. So it was best to avoid talking to Mom until she'd had some rest and could control her emotions.

A phone rang downstairs. A few minutes later, there was a knock on her door.

She opened it to find Sawyer standing there, his cell phone at his ear.

"It's Heath." He held the phone out to her, his eyes searching her face. "When you're finished, dinner's ready."

She accepted the phone. "Thanks. I'll be right there."

Closing the door, she crossed to the bed and sat, her heart racing. "Hello?"

"I wanted to check on you. Make sure you're okay."

The sound of his voice made her heart soar.

"I'm truly sorry about what happened this morning," he continued. "I never would've climbed up the mountain if I'd thought Larry and Joe were close by."

"We agreed, no more apologizing. Besides, you saved me." She traced the pattern of the patch-work quilt. "Did you catch Larry?"

"No." A heavy sigh sounded across the line. She could almost see the frown marring his hand-some face. "But I don't want you to worry. We *will* catch him."

"I know you will. You have Joe. So that's something."

There was a long pause. She held her breath. What was he not telling her? Had Joe escaped?

"Just promise me you'll be careful. Be extra aware of your surroundings. Until we catch Larry."

"Of course... You don't think he'll come after me, do you? I mean what would be the purpose? It's not like I'm a member of law enforcement. I can't put him in jail or anything. I'm nothing to him." She knew she was rambling but couldn't seem to control it. Why would Larry target her specifically? "Wouldn't it be wiser for him to leave the area? Go on the run? It's not like I did anything that would cause him to have a vendetta against me."

"I don't disagree with you. But, please, humor me...take all the precautions you can."

"I always do." *Believe me, I learned the dangers of the world from one of the evilest men ever to have walked the earth.*

"Okay. I'll check in with you tomorrow."

"You don't have my number."

"You obviously underestimate my investigative powers." Rich laughter came across the line. "Your brother promised to forward your number to me, if you're okay with him doing so. That was the main reason I called him. I was glad to find out you were there and I could hear your voice."

For the first time since she'd accepted the job in Barton Creek, Kayla's heart felt lighter. Though she didn't understand why. "I'm glad you called. I've…" Would he read too much into the comment if she said she'd been worried about him? "Try to get some sleep tonight. I'm sure you got very little last night. I know you want to catch Larry quickly, but you need to take care of yourself, too."

The sound of him clearing his throat passed through the line. "I've gotta go. Enjoy your family time. And, Kayla…"

"Yes?"

"Try not to worry and get some rest." The line went dead.

Why had he ended the conversation so suddenly? Had she crossed a boundary when she'd admitted she'd been concerned about his safety? No. That didn't sound like Heath. He wasn't someone who'd take a comment like that as a personal attack against his ability to protect himself. Or was he? Could he be a man who needed to feel like a puffed-up hero? She had no clue.

*Face it, girl, when it comes to men, you do not have what it takes to pick a good one.*

All the more reason to live out her life alone.

Heath pinched the bridge of his nose and bowed his head. He'd been so happy to hear Kayla's voice and know she was safe, but when she'd expressed her concern for his well-being, it was as if someone had doused him with a bucket of ice water. He had spent his career purposefully keeping women outside law enforcement at arm's length. If he was worried about causing some-one—a close friend, girlfriend, wife—distress, he would not be as focused on the job at hand as he should be. When officers got sloppy with their work, people got hurt.

"You okay, boss?"

"I'm fine." Heath glanced up to see Deputy Bishop standing in his office doorway. "Did you need something?"

"Yeah. I was going to let you know they've ID our John Doe. The federal agents requested the medical examiner take the deceased person's fingerprints. When we ran them through the da-tabase, we got a hit. His name is Ray Anderson. Age fifty-three. He's from Robbinsville, North Carolina."

"Did you notify the sheriff over in Graham County?"

"I did. He said Ray was a hermit of sorts. No family. He worked as a mechanic at L&J Auto."

"Let me guess. L&J Auto is owned by Larry and Joe."

"You got it. Larry Frye and Joe Granger. Broth-ers-in-law. Joe is married to Larry's sister. Larry inherited the business from his dad, who passed away three years ago, and then he brought Joe on as a partner."

"See if the Graham County sheriff can send you a photo of Larry and let's get it circulated. The sooner we catch him, the happier I'll be."

"Already done. Also, he plans to keep an eye on the business and Larry's home in case he returns."

"What about Joe's house? Larry could go to his sister for help."

Deputy Bishop glanced at his small notebook. "Larry's sister, Brenda, will be brought in for questioning, and Sheriff Howard said to let you know to expect a call from him tomorrow."

"Thanks, Bishop." Heath rolled his shoulders and turned toward his computer. Time to see what he could find out about Larry Frye.

"Sir." Deputy Bishop remained in the doorway.

"Yeah," Heath queried as he entered his computer passcode.

"If I may say so, don't you think it'd be wise if you went home? Got a shower and a few hours' sleep."

"What?" He looked at his deputy, concern etched on his face.

"I don't mean to overstep boundaries, but you have spent the past week on a hiking trail—the last thirty-six hours trying to apprehend criminals. You must be exhausted."

"Yes, but I—"

"Have control issues and don't know when to take a break," Parker interjected, pushing past the deputy. "It's okay, Deputy. I've got it from here."

Heath's brother walked into his office and closed the door behind him.

"If you're here to check up on me, there's no need. I'm fine," Heath declared before Parker could sit down.

"I know that." He dropped into one of the leather armchairs positioned in front of Heath's desk. "I just wanted to hear how things went. Have y'all captured your guy?"

"Not yet."

"I'm not surprised. Even with rangers and federal agents out there looking. There are too many places to hide when you get off the trail and go into the woods."

"I guess. Of course, we're still thinking he may have hitched a ride out of the park." Heath scratched his chin. Shaving would be the first thing on his to-do list when he made it home. "You'll have to wait for my report on the gear I tested on my trip. This case has to take precedence."

"No worries." Parker leaned forward. "Listen, I know you're the sheriff and you know how to take care of yourself, but don't pull a stunt like that again. Going off into the wilderness when you're past the brink of exhaustion and don't have adequate backup."

"I had Sawyer. He's a trained agent."

"Yeah, well. I think you were both reckless. Larry could have been waiting in the bushes and taken you both out as you dropped off the side of the mountain."

"You worry too much, little brother. Besides, we all made it out of there." Heath looked Parker in the eyes. "A big part of that is thanks to you. I couldn't have chased after Larry if you hadn't been there to help. I knew you'd get Kayla out of there safely. That was a big worry off my shoulders."

Parker narrowed his eyes, making Heath uncomfortable. What was his younger brother thinking?

Several long minutes passed with neither man saying a word. Finally, Parker pushed to his feet. "Guess I need to get home. If Mom sees me, what do you want me to tell her?"

"Why would you need to tell her anything?"

"You know news in this town spreads faster than soft butter on hot toast. I guarantee she'll be watching for me, just so she can probe me for answers." Parker shoved his hand through his hair. "I really need to find a place of my own soon. Renting the apartment above Mom and Dad's garage seemed like a good idea, but it's actually been very stressful trying to avoid all of Mom's questions about my dating life and career choices."

Laughter bubbled up inside Heath and his chest shook. "I tried to warn you. Told you what it would be like, but you said home-cooked meals would more than make up for any of Mom's nosy tendencies."

"I stand by that statement. Home-cooked meals would make up for it, but Mom's on a new diet that consists of protein shakes and salads." Parker frowned.

The laughter he'd tried to suppress exploded from Heath. He stood and rounded his desk to face his brother. "I suggest you stop at a fast-food restaurant on your way home. And if Mom does corner you about me, tell her the fine citizens of Blount County trusted me enough to elect me to this job. She needs to accept that I'm a grown man, capable of taking care of my own business. Then give her a kiss for me and tell her I'll see her in a few days."

"You got it." Parker clapped him on the shoulder. "For the record, I'm glad you're okay, and I hope you can get a good night's rest."

*Me, too.* Though he was doubtful that would happen. He might have one killer sitting in jail tonight, but he still had another one on the loose. He wouldn't truly rest until he captured Larry Frye.

# ELEVEN

"Yes. Thank you. I will be there within the hour." Kayla disconnected the call.

Bridget poked her head into the guest bedroom. "Where will you be within the hour?"

"Oh, hi. I thought you'd left for the office." She had always marveled at her sister-in-law's ability to juggle family life and a full-time career as a top-notch bodyguard and manager of the Knoxville branch of the security firm Protective Instincts—co-owned by her brother Ryan Vincent and his best friend Lincoln James.

"I decided to take the day off so I could spend some time with you." Bridget walked into the room and sat on the foot of the bed. "I'm sorry. I really wasn't trying to eavesdrop. You had the door open and I was walking past…"

"It's okay. It wasn't a private conversation or anything. I was arranging for a rental car. And I was hoping Sawyer could drive me."

Sawyer entered the room, Vincent in his

arms. The instant the toddler saw his mommy, he reached out and leaned toward her. Bridget laughed and held out her hands. He dove into her lap, giggling. Sawyer kissed the top of his wife's head and then turned to face his sister. "Where do you need me to drive you?"

Kayla swallowed the pang of envy that welled up inside her. She wasn't jealous of her brother's happiness, just sad that she would never experience the same. Although, she had to admit, if anyone deserved the true fairy tale, it was Sawyer. He'd been raised by a single mom, who'd struggled to support him, while Kayla had been raised in a home with two loving parents and had never wanted for anything. She would never understand how her father could walk away from his firstborn child, and there was nothing she could do to take away the feeling of abandonment Sawyer had felt growing up. But she could—and always would—celebrate the life her brother had built in spite of the circumstances of his early years. She knew the man who raised her in a loving two-parent home was a changed man from the one who walked away from his first marriage and son. The remorse her dad had displayed in the later years of his life and his great desire to be reunited with his son had been the motivation that had pushed her to continue looking for Sawyer even after her dad had lost his battle with cancer. And she was thankful she had persistently pursued the relationship. Her big brother's love was a true blessing.

"Kayla…" Sawyer peered at her, his brow creasing.

"Oh." She shook her head, clearing her thoughts. "I need a lift to the car rental place on Wisteria Street."

"There's no need for you to be out the expense of a rental."

"My insurance will cover the cost."

"But Bridget can drive you to the clinic each morning on her way to Knoxville. I'll pick you up each evening."

He couldn't be serious. She pushed out a breath and prepared to tell him what she thought of his plan. Before she could say anything, Bridget bound to her feet, grasped her husband's shirtsleeve and turned him toward the door.

"Your sister is a grown woman. She doesn't need you planning her schedule for her."

"I know, but—"

"You love her and you want her safe. We all do." Bridget popped up onto her tiptoes and kissed her husband's cheek. "Trust her to make her own choices. Go grab your keys. She'll be right out."

"I was being a bulldozer again, huh?"

"Just a tiny bit."

Sawyer locked eyes with Kayla. "I'll be ready

to go in ten minutes." He kissed his son's cheek and turned and walked out of the room.

"How did you do that?" Kayla asked in awe. "I've never seen him so agreeable."

A smile lit Bridget's face as she bounced Vincent on her hip. "You forget. I grew up with five brothers, all of whom—even the two who were younger than me—wanted to treat me like a child who needed to be protected." A sadness clouded her eyes. "It wasn't until I almost lost my life to Lovelorn that they realized I was no longer the *little* sister who needed them to fight my battles."

A pain stabbed Kayla's chest. She swallowed the gasp that wanted to escape. Would she ever be able to hear the name the media had dubbed Jonathan during his killing spree without feeling both physical and mental pain? Probably not. She had loved him. There was no denying it, or convincing herself otherwise. The version of Jonathan she'd known had been quirky and spontaneous and someone who'd enjoyed debating current events. He had treated her with respect and made her feel protected. That was why she'd happily said yes when he'd proposed to her. Two days later, the man she'd loved had transformed into a monster right before her eyes and she'd spent the next five days living in a nightmare.

Her near-death experience had only heightened her family's desire to protect her. Although she knew her mother's and brother's actions were done out of love and concern, she felt suffocated by their constant need to check on her. Would she ever reach the point where she could kindly point out their overbearing behaviors the way Bridget had with Sawyer just now?

If she remembered correctly, her sister-in-law had survived a previous attack several months prior to Jonathan's attempt on her life. And she was one of the strongest, most independent women Kayla knew.

"You seem deep in thought," Bridget observed.

"I'm just thinking about how much I admire you. I wish I could be just like you—a fearless, resilient woman."

"Oh, sweet sister, I am far from fearless. I want to tell you a little secret… Everyone has their own challenges to work through. Most of the time, those challenges are a daily struggle. From my perspective, you are doing amazing." Bridget sat on the bed, with Vincent on her lap staring wide-eyed at Kayla. "I was afraid the ordeal of being trapped in the woods with killers would be too much for you and you would withdraw into your shell. But I was wrong. Look at you. This morning, you've dealt with the insurance company and arranged for a replacement vehicle. And if I'm not mistaken, you plan to move into your cabin rental today and start work tomorrow?"

"Well, I don't really have a choice, do I? I came to Barton Creek to do a job. How would it look if I hid out at my brother's house and refused to help the people who need me?"

Bridget swept Kayla into a big hug, a giggling Vincent caught in the middle. Tears welled in Kayla's eyes. "I always wanted a sister," she whispered.

"Me, too. I'm thankful God gave me you." Bridget pulled back. "If you need me, I'm only a phone call away. Got it?"

Unable to get words past the lump in her throat, Kayla bobbed her head up and down.

"It's time I put this little one down for a nap. Try not to give your brother a hard time on the ride to the rental place. He has a good heart and means well."

"I know."

Bridget hummed a lullaby and waltzed out of the room. Time to face her big brother and break the news that, while she appreciated his hospitality, she was moving into her rental today. Snagging her purse off the dresser, she plastered a smile on her face and headed for the door.

Closing his eyes, Heath rubbed his temples. He had spent the morning interrogating Joe, who had lawyered up and only given minimal answers. To top that off, the joint K-9 unit Heath and the FBI agents had sent into the woods late yesterday to track Larry hadn't been able to pick up the killer's trail. And they'd had to be pulled off the job just after noon to assist in the search of a toddler that had wandered away from her family on a camping trip. They'd located the young child within three hours and had reunited her with her grateful parents. While he was thankful his officers had found the toddler, unharmed, he couldn't help but worry that Larry could be in his town hunting him and Kayla. Thankfully, he knew Sawyer would keep Kayla safe, taking one burden off his shoulders. *Burden? No. Keeping Kayla safe would not be a burden.* If he were being honest with himself, he'd missed her these past twenty-four hours and had spent much of the day resisting the urge to call and hear her voice.

Heath's phone rang, startling him. Sawyer's name flashed on the screen. "Sawyer, what's up?"

"Heath, I hate to ask, but could you have your deputies drive past Kayla's rental cabin at regular intervals overnight? I wanted Bridget to assign a bodyguard to stand guard outside but neither she nor Kayla would hear of it. Honestly, I don't know what they're thinking. She could have just stayed here." Sawyer paused and took a deep breath. His unusual talkativeness punctuated Sawyer's frustration. In this moment, he sounded more like his loquacious wife than the reserved profiler Heath knew.

"Wait a minute. Kayla's not at your house?"

"No. She rented a car this morning, checked in at the clinic—with plans to start work tomorrow—and moved into the cabin she's renting from Mrs. Frances."

Heath's grip tightened on the phone and he pushed to his feet. "Why would she leave your house before we caught Larry?"

"She said that she had withdrawn after Jonathan tried to kill her and she refuses to do so again. I have to respect her strength, but her stubbornness and refusal to even bend, just a little, is another matter."

Heath could have easily pointed out to his friend that Sawyer and his sister shared the same stubborn trait but chose not to. "Well, what's done is done. I'll have my deputies drive by the area every hour overnight. Also, I don't live far from there, so I can reach her within minutes. I'll touch base with her and make sure she knows to call me if anything happens."

"Thank you." A heavy sigh sounded across the line. "I had really hoped you would tell me you'd captured Larry and the threat was over."

"Unfortunately, he's evaded us so far. I had to pull my K9 unit from the search. However, we've been able to identify him and the deceased person. The sheriff in North Carolina has officers keeping watch on the auto shop Larry and Joe own, as well as his home. Just in case he shows up at one of those places. We've also issued a be-on-the-lookout order statewide. If he shows up, we'll get him."

"I pray that's sooner, rather than later."

*Me, too.* "I'll let you know when he's in custody. Text me the cabin number for Kayla's rental." Heath disconnected the call. His phone dinged immediately and he glanced at the text from Sawyer.

The paperwork on Heath's desk had piled up during his weeklong vacation. He really needed to spend a couple more hours in his office catching up. But an overwhelming urge to check on Kayla and see her face-to-face welled up inside him. The paperwork would wait. He grabbed his keys and sprinted out of his office.

Thirty-five minutes later, he pulled to a stop in front of Kayla's cabin. As he'd suspected when he'd seen the address, Kayla had rented the most remote cabin on the property. The Hideaway Inn Bed and Breakfast—which comprised of ten rooms inside the inn that were rented by the night and four small cabins scattered around the property that were rented by the week or month—had been owned and operated by Frances Nolan— Mrs. Frances to the locals—a retired librarian, for the past twenty years. During that time there had been no disturbances on the property that required the police to respond. Heath prayed that would not change now.

A blue compact car sat in the short driveway. He snagged the pizza box off the front seat and exited his vehicle. As he approached the cabin, the front door flew open. Kayla stood framed in the doorway, a hand on her hip and a frown on her face. "Did my brother send you to check on me?"

He laughed. "Not exactly. He asked that I have my deputies keep an extra eye out in this area overnight. Stopping by was my idea." He held up the pizza box. "I didn't know if you'd had time to buy groceries. Since I was craving pizza, I thought I could share."

Several seconds passed but finally she smiled. "Pepperoni, mushrooms and black olives? With extra cheese?"

"Is there any other kind?"

Kayla stepped back and opened the door wide. "How did you know my favorite kind of pizza? Did you ask Sawyer?" she asked as he entered the cabin.

"I didn't." He grinned and shrugged. "I bought my favorite, with the idea that you could pick off anything you didn't like."

Her melodic laughter filled the space. For the first time since he'd answered his phone and heard that she had left the safety of her brother's home, Heath felt part of the weight lift off his shoulders.

*Dear Lord, please let me keep this amazing*

*woman safe.* He silently summoned the prayer that he had repeated numerous times since the moment he'd first met her.

# TWELVE

Kayla opened a cabinet and removed two plates, thankful that Mrs. Nolan had outfitted her cabins with all the household essentials. Kayla hadn't been expecting company. However, she had stopped at the grocery store on her way home from the clinic and had picked up a few items.

She placed the plates onto the table and turned to Heath. "I'm sorry. I don't have any cola, but I have milk, water or unsweet tea. Which would you prefer?"

"Unsweet tea? Don't you know you're in the South now? We like our tea extra sweet." Heath laughed.

"I'll keep that in mind for next time." Heat crept up her neck. Why had she said that? He'd think she was expecting dinner with him to become a routine thing.

"It's okay. I prefer water anyway."

He settled the pizza on the center of the table and lifted the lid. The aroma of tomato sauce and melted cheese instantly filled the room, causing Kayla's stomach to growl.

She giggled. "I guess I'm hungrier than I realized. I have been on the go all day and haven't taken time to eat since breakfast."

"Then I'm doubly glad that I decided to swing by and see you. We can't have you starving."

She sat in the chair opposite him at the small table. He held out his hand, palm upward. "Do you mind if I say grace?"

A lump formed in her throat. She placed her hand in his, nodded and bowed her head. Her relationship with God had struggled for a few years following her ordeal with Jonathan, but she'd been working to rebuild it. The blessings in her life were something she never wanted to take for granted and giving thanks would always be important to her, no matter the situation she found herself in.

"Thank You, Lord, for guiding us out of the wilderness unharmed, for new friendships and for this food we are about to eat. Lord, we pray that this food is nourishing to our bodies and that we will always live our lives for You. In Christ's name, amen."

He glanced up, smiled, let go of her hand and reached for a large slice of pizza. Then he plopped it onto her plate, repeating the process for himself. "If you've never had pizza from Mama Mary's Pizzeria, you are in for a treat."

"You realize I went to college in New York City, right? I had easy access to the best pizzas in the world."

He picked up his slice and nodded toward her plate. "You be the judge." Then he took a big bite. "Mmm."

She smiled, bit into her own slice and savored it. "Oh, my, this is so good."

Heath chuckled. "Mary Rossi and her husband, Carlo, moved here a few years ago after they retired from… New York City, where they ran a family pizzeria for thirty years. Within six months of arriving in Barton Creek, they realized they were happier in the kitchen than they were fishing or playing golf, so they opened a restaurant. And I, for one, am very thankful they did."

"I never would've dreamed of getting a New York-style pizza in Tennessee."

"You might be surprised what Tennessee has to offer."

*Like men that were gentlemen.* Now, where had that thought come from? The heat that had crept up her neck earlier spread into her cheeks. She gulped her water and prayed Heath didn't ask her why she was turning red.

They ate in silence until two-thirds of the pizza had been consumed. She was stuffed.

Heath leaned against the back of his chair. "If I may ask, without seeming to be too nosy, why didn't you stay at Sawyer and Bridget's house, at least for one more night?"

They had finished the meal, so it was time for the interrogation. No. After spending thirty hours in the woods with the man sitting across from her, she knew his question came from a place of concern. It was not his intention to imply she was incapable of taking care of herself.

She pushed back her chair and stood. "Let me find a container to put the pizza in so you can take the leftovers home. Then we can sit on the sofa. And I'll answer your questions."

"Oh, no." He shook his head. "You get to keep the leftovers. That way, I'll know you've been fed." He smiled at her, his eyes sparkling.

"Are you sure? Because I won't turn it down. There's nothing I love more than cold pizza for breakfast."

"Good. Enjoy."

"If you want to move to the sofa, I'll be right there."

"Can't I help with the cleanup?"

She giggled. "In this tiny space? No way. Besides, there's not much. Now, go."

He did as she asked and Kayla put away the food. Then she stacked their dishes and placed them into the sink. They could wait until later. Crossing to the sofa, she looked around the room. The cabin had an open-concept main area, a bathroom and one bedroom. It was small, but it was perfect for her. As long as she could push away her fears that Larry would find her, she knew she could be very happy here.

She sat on the opposite end of the sofa, one leg tucked underneath her. "After I left the hospital following Jonathan's attempt on my life, I went home to stay with my mother in Virginia. I couldn't face going back to my apartment in New York where Jonathan and I had hung out, watched movies, cooked meals and planned our future." Sadness washed over her. "It took me two months, five days and six hours to step outside of the house for the first time. I will never forget the fear I felt that day. Mom had convinced me to walk to the mailbox."

Her mom's voice echoed in her mind. *It's forty feet. You need fresh air and sunshine.*

"I made it halfway to the mailbox, turned around and ran back indoors."

"What startled you?" Heath asked softly.

"A car drove past. I had an overwhelming fear it was someone who wanted to hurt me." She lowered her head and peeked at him through her lashes. There was no expression of judgment on his face as he waited for her to continue.

"After that, I finally agreed to meet with a counselor. Three months later, I moved back to my apartment and enrolled in my final semester at NYU. My roommate and friends were wonderful. They walked with me to classes and made sure someone was with me most of the time. Four and a half months later, I graduated with my Bachelor of Science in Nursing. I accepted a job in a general-practice office and started working on my master's degree. For two years, I spent my life working, going to school or sleeping, with no time for anything else.

"Six months ago, my counselor helped me to realize, while I'd been busy—leading a seemingly productive life—what I'd really been doing was hiding. My friends all moved on with their lives, most of them getting married and having children. While I don't seek to have any of those things, I also don't want my life to be stagnant any longer. Which is why I became a traveling nurse. This is my first assignment." She met his gaze. "Leaving the comfort of my apartment and my mundane job was supposed to lead me to new adventures."

He picked up her hand that rested on the seat cushion. And for the first time since Jonathan, she didn't flinch or pull away… No, not the first time. She hadn't pulled away when he'd held her hand in the woods. *You were running for your life.* Or when he'd held her as she'd cried and fallen asleep in his arms the night they'd slept under the tree against the mountain. *You were frightened and he offered comfort. Nothing more.* Kayla could not explain her reaction to this man.

Had she become comfortable with the sheriff? Even though she didn't want a romantic relationship, could they build a friendship? It might be nice to have a friend. Especially in Barton Creek.

"I imagine when you were thinking of having adventures, you weren't planning on anything like what you got," he said softly.

"Hardly. I was mainly thinking about visiting unknown places and trying out different restaurants."

"I'm kind of surprised you chose to come to Barton Creek, considering your history here."

"I also have family here. And a nephew I want to spend more time with."

"That makes sense." He raised an eyebrow. "But that leads me back to my original question. Why didn't you stay with Sawyer and Bridget?"

She moistened her lips, gently tugged her hand free from his and looked down at her lap. "I wanted to. Desperately. However, I was afraid, if I did, my fears would take over again. It would be a repeat of the last time. I'm not sure I could ever come back from something like that again."

Kayla closed her eyes and waited for his response. Would he think she was weak and needed to get a better grip on her emotions? Other than her counselor, and Bridget, no one else truly knew how deeply scarred she was emotionally. How completely paralyzing her fear had been following Jonathan.

\* \* \*

Her willingness to be totally raw and vulnerable in front of Heath touched his heart in such a way that he wanted to sweep her into his arms and tell her everything was going to be okay. That she was safe and that she was one of the strongest people had ever met. But he needed to tread lightly. When he had taken her hand in his earlier, she had pulled back. He couldn't have her thinking he was offering anything more than friendship.

"Why didn't you explain all of this to Sawyer? Your brother loves you. He would have understood. And may have been able to help you—"

"Help me?" Kayla lifted her head and pinned him with her gaze. "Don't you understand? This isn't something that can be *fixed* by a well-meaning family member or friend. And if you know my brother at all, you know that's exactly what he'd try to do."

Heath had no doubt she was correct. After all, Sawyer had been bullheaded enough to venture into the wilderness in the middle of the night, during a flash flood, to rescue his sister. Although Heath couldn't say he blamed him. If he had a sister, he would have done the same thing.

"Isn't your brother trained in psychology? He was a prominent profiler for the FBI. Wouldn't he understand, better than most people, how to hel—" He'd almost said *help* but realized his error and swallowed the word before it could escape. "How to guide you?"

She offered him a half smile. "I appreciate your desire to *help*. I also understand why you and Sawyer think I'd be better off at his house, where he and Bridget can guard me. Unfortunately, this is something I have to work through on my own."

"I get that. But what about Larry? We haven't captured him yet."

"You said yourself he's not from this area. Well, I'm not either. Only a couple of people even know I'm in town. I don't start at the clinic until Monday. Which gives you roughly sixty hours to catch Larry before the rest of the population in Barton Creek finds out I'm here."

"I thought you were starting at the clinic tomorrow?"

"I had planned to, but Dr. Lester decided I needed an extra day to rest after my ordeal." She shrugged. "Since she's the boss, I didn't know how to turn down the offer. So I thought I would do a little shopping. Maybe even venture into Gatlinburg and check out a few tourist attractions."

Heath didn't like the idea of her wandering around alone. Realistically, he knew she should be fine in a crowded location like Gatlinburg, especially this time of year, but still. He wouldn't be completely comfortable about her safety until Larry was in custody.

"I'll go with you," he blurted before he could stop and think through his actions. "That is...*if* you would like, I would be happy to accompany you and be your tour guide."

Was she blushing? Did she think he meant it to be a date? "You said yourself Sawyer can be overly protective. If he finds out you've gone off on your own, he'll have a bodyguard at your doorstep before you return."

"Bridget wouldn't allow that," she insisted.

"Do you think your sister-in-law is the only person in the greater Knoxville area that runs a security firm? If your brother decides you need a guard, he'll hire one from another company if Bridget won't assign a Protective Instincts' bodyguard to the job."

Kayla sighed and leaned back against the sofa. "You're probably right. But I can't let you take a day off to babysit me. You just returned from your vacation. I'm sure you have a lot of work to catch up on."

"First, I wouldn't be babysitting. Second, I have a lot of unused paid time off. Taking another day won't be a big deal." He crossed his fingers behind his back—a silly childhood ritual that one did when they told a fib—something he hadn't done since he was eight years old. What he'd said had been the truth, so why'd he feel like it was a lie? *Because you have a lot of paperwork to sort through and your officers have worked overtime covering while you were on vacation.*

Taking tomorrow off would mean asking a deputy to come in on their day off. No matter. He'd make it work. He was the boss, after all. *Except you promised you'd never use the fact that you're the boss to get your way.* Especially not at the expense of your employees.

He met Kayla's gaze. She quirked an eyebrow but remained silent. Suddenly, he felt like an awkward teenager who'd asked the most popular girl in school to the movies. "I, um, I'm sorry. I didn't mean to overstep. Or imply that you *had* to let me go with you."

"I know I don't *have to* let you but…" She fidgeted with her hands. "It would be nice to have a tour guide. If you're sure I won't be keeping you from something."

Her hazel eyes shimmered with hope and Heath knew in that instant there was nowhere he'd rather be than sightseeing with her. Even shopping didn't sound as excruciating as it normally did. What was going on with him? *Nothing.*

He'd put her in this dangerous situation. It was his responsibility to keep an eye on her, to ensure her safety. When it came right down to it, accompanying her tomorrow *was* part of his job. He was protecting a visitor to his county.

"Okay then." Heath stood. "I guess I should get going. Thank you for your hospitality."

Kayla bound to her feet. "No. *Thank you* for bringing pizza. I'll buy lunch tomorrow to repay the favor."

"I'll pick you up in the morning. How does nine thirty sound?"

"Nine thirty is fine. I'll be ready."

"Okay." He glanced around the small cabin. "I'll check the back door and windows before I leave. Make sure they're all locked and secure." Heath turned back to her. "That is, if you don't mind?"

*Please, Lord, let her say yes. I need to feel like she's safe here or I won't be able to sleep tonight.*

"Go ahead." She smiled and swept her arm wide. "Then you can report back to Sawyer and let him know I am fine."

He wanted to tell her he wouldn't do that, but even he knew it would be a lie. So, instead, he whistled a tune under his breath and worked his way through the entire cabin, checking the locks on the windows in the living and dining area, bedroom, bathroom and the back door leading to the small deck. Then he returned to where she waited. "Everything's locked up tight. You have my number?"

"Yes."

"Promise me, if you get frightened or have a feeling that something is wrong, you'll call me. I only live a few miles away and can be here in under five minutes."

"I promise." She searched his face. "Be honest with me. What are the odds that Larry will find me here?"

"Honest? I'd say they're slim. Blount County covers a lot of area. He doesn't know your last name, and even if he did, he wouldn't find an address for you since you aren't a resident of the county." Heath placed his hands on her shoulders. "But that doesn't mean you should let down your guard. Understand?"

She nodded, her lips turning down at the corners.

He drew her into a tight embrace. "I'm sorry I put you in this situation. If I had known the driver of the vehicle was you and what the result of my actions would be, I never would have never run into the road."

Kayla returned his embrace and, for a brief moment, the stress he'd been feeling lifted from him. All too soon, she pulled away. "I'll see you in the morning. Wear comfortable shoes."

He looked at her Converse-clad feet. "I believe you need to heed your own advice. Do you have any other kind of shoe?"

Laughter erupted from her. "Of course, I do. And I will wear appropriate shoes tomorrow."

"Good night, then." He stepped onto the small porch, closed the door behind him and listened until he heard the dead bolt slide into place.

Pulling his phone out of his pocket, he headed to his vehicle. Dispatch answered on the second ring. "Tell the on-duty deputy to patrol the area around Hideaway Inn Bed and Breakfast hourly, paying extra attention to cabin number four. Also, I'll expect a text update every hour." He disconnected the call and looked back at the cabin one last time. "Lord, please, keep her safe."

# THIRTEEN

Heath pulled into the small driveway, parked his SUV behind Kayla's rental car for the second night in a row and turned off the engine.

"There's no need for you to get out." Kayla reached for her door handle.

"Stay put," he commanded. "I'll come around and open the door for you. Your arms are a little full."

She giggled. "I did kind of overspend today. But how could I resist the outlet stores in Sevierville? Who knew they had such bargains?"

He jogged around the vehicle. Accepting two of the three bags she had balanced on her lap, he stepped back and held the door while she exited the SUV. Then he reached into the back seat and grabbed the larger bag that had been resting on the floorboard. "I'll carry these. That way, you can open the door of the cabin without having to juggle packages while trying to wrestle with the lock."

Once they entered the house, they both deposited their packages on the dining table. Kayla instantly started pulling things out of the bags like a little kid at Christmas, a smile on her face. Her joy was evident, even though she knew what was inside each bag.

"I'll check through the house. Make sure everything is secure. Then get out of your way."

Kayla glanced up, a shoebox in her hand. "Do you think that's necessary? The cabin is less than six hundred square feet. Where would anyone hide?"

"I don't know. But I'll feel better after I check."

She shrugged one shoulder and dug back into the sack she'd pulled the shoebox out of. "Okay. If you insist."

Starting in the bedroom, Heath repeated the process from the night before and checked all the windows and the back door. The cabin was secure.

"Everything good?" She raised an eyebrow.

"Yes, but remember, call me if anything spooks you."

The smile that she'd been wearing most of the day reached her eyes. "The only thing I heard last night was a couple of raccoons and a possum on the deck. So, I think I'm safe. But *thank you.* For going with me today and for checking to make sure no one had breached the cabin. It's nice to have a friend."

Crossing to the stove, she picked up the teakettle and filled it with water from the faucet. Then she returned the kettle to the stove and turned on the burner. "Would you like some tea? Or coffee?"

*Would you like some tea? Or coffee?* That was a resounding yes. He couldn't remember the last time he had enjoyed spending the day with someone as much as he had today. Unfortunately, he planned to work a few hours tonight to get caught up on some of the paperwork he'd put off to spend time with her. "No, thank you. I need to get going. Make sure you lock up behind me."

"Of course. Believe me, my brother has trained me well. And I keep my personal alarm and pepper spray beside the bed at night."

He hated that the evil of this world had touched her, not once but twice. It was one thing to take precautions, but it was another to live in fear.

She walked him to the door and they stood there awkwardly for a moment. Should he shake her hand or hug her goodbye as he had the night before? He'd never really been much of a hugger with women outside of his family. How did one end a date? No, not a date. Just an outing with a friend who was a woman.

"I enjoyed the day. Thanks for—" His phone rang. He pulled it out of his pocket. Deputy Moore's name flashed on the screen. *Saved by the bell.*

"Sorry, I have to take this." He held up the phone, swiped to answer and put it to his ear.

"Thanks for a fun day," she whispered and opened the door for him.

He smiled, walked out the door, pausing briefly to listen to the door lock click into place before jogging to his SUV. "Sheriff Dalton."

"Sheriff. We got a lead on Larry. Mrs. Sue at the diner said someone came in asking questions. He described Kayla, asking if anyone knew how he could get in touch with her. He also asked questions about you."

"She didn't tell him anything, did she?"

"No, sir. You know Sue. Being a retired dispatcher, she knows better than to give out personal information. However, she recognized the description of Kayla. That's why she called me. He must've gotten nervous about his food taking so long to arrive and he took off before we got there."

"Thanks for the info. I'll swing by the diner and talk to Sue on my way back to the office. Radio the deputy on patrol and tell him to increase his patrol around The Hideaway Inn Bed and Breakfast. I want him to check the area surrounding Kayla's cabin every half hour. And tell him to make sure he's not being followed. I wouldn't put it past Larry to be driving around following police officers and trying to see if one would lead him to me or Kayla."

"Yes, sir."

Heath disconnected the call and briefly wondered if he should call Kayla and warn her. No. It would serve no purpose except to cause her to worry.

Ten minutes later, he pulled into the diner's parking lot and circled the building, looking for any vehicles that seemed out of place. The bell over the door dinged when he entered the restaurant. Sue glanced up from behind the counter, where she stood refilling a customer's coffee. With a slight jerk of her head, she motioned for him to go into the kitchen. He discreetly went through the swinging double doors, waved at the fry cook, and slipped into the small office in the back of the building.

"Well, well, Sheriff," Sue said, entering the tiny room. "The man that was in here asking questions earlier must be mighty important for you to come question me yourself."

Heath accepted a motherly hug from his favorite former dispatcher. "I'm just thankful he stopped in your restaurant. Someone else may have inadvertently given him too many answers. He didn't realize he was dealing with a shrewd woman with police connections."

She laughed. "I took out the trash and got a look at his vehicle as he was driving away. It was an old, beat-up truck. Green, with a rusted front fender on the right side. Mud covered the tag, so I wasn't able to get the numbers, but it was a North Carolina license plate."

"Thank you. I doubt he will, but if he comes back—"

"I'll call you."

"Thanks." He kissed her cheek. "I've got to go."

"Let me send some supper with you," she called after him. "How about meatloaf, mashed potatoes and turnip greens?"

"Sounds delicious, but I've already eaten. I promise to come back soon."

"Make sure you bring Kayla Eldridge with you."

He turned and met her gaze. "Why would you think Kayla and I would have dinner together?"

"Just a feeling. The few times I've seen that girl in town, in recent years, she looked like she could use a good meal."

Heath shook his head and headed for the door, her laughter echoing behind him.

*Thank you, Lord, for small towns and people who look out for their neighbors.*

Kayla rolled over and readjusted her pillow for the tenth time in as many minutes. Until this point, she had spent her entire career in the same doctor's office in the city. Excitement and anxiousness combined to create a nervous energy that zinged through her. Following the Sunday morning church service, she'd report to the clinic for her first day as a travel nurse. It almost felt like the night before the first day of school after summer break. She glanced at the clock: 1:13 a.m. She had been tossing and turning for two and a half hours. Her alarm would go off at six thirty. Kayla sighed. Tossing and turning in bed wasn't helping her get to sleep any faster. Maybe a cup of warm milk would help.

She pushed back the covers and froze. There was a sound at the back door. Could it be the raccoons from the night before? Were they searching for food? The knob rattled and something, or someone, pushed against the door. Her breath caught. That wasn't a wild animal.

Her heart pounded in her chest. Palm flat, she felt on the bedside table, searching until her fingers touched her key ring and phone. Grasping them, she held her breath and listened. All was quiet. Could it have been her imagination?

After listening a few more minutes, she shoved her feet into her slippers and made her way to the open bedroom door. Leaving the lights off, she took a half step through the doorway and paused. Silence.

The door that led to the back deck was to the left, less than ten feet away. She took a step toward it. Maybe, if she peeked through the blinds covering the window in the door, she'd see the raccoons and it would ease her nerves.

Kayla inched forward and lifted her hand—
the doorknob jiggled. A man's silhouette was
outlined on the blinds. She jumped back, slamming against the hall wall, stuck a knuckle in her
mouth and bit it—hard—to suppress the scream
that burned for release. She pressed against the
wall and worked her way along the short hallway, darted into the bedroom, closing and latch-
ing the door. Then she pulled the accent chair in
front of it.

Sinking to the floor in front of the chair, she
dialed Heath's number. The doorknob jiggling
becoming louder. The man outside was no longer trying to hide his presence.

"Kayla? What's wrong? Are you okay?" Heath
shot out questions in rapid succession, his voice
husky from sleep.

"There's someone here… Trying to break in
the back door. I'm scared." She heard movement
in the background, across the phone line. "I'm
on my way."

Banging echoed throughout the tiny cabin as
the person repeatedly hit the back door, trying to
break it open. "Heath, are you still there?"

"Yes. I was sending a text to Deputy Fisher.
He's on his way." The sound of Heath getting
into his SUV came through the phone. "Where
are you?"

"I'm in the bedroom. I locked the door and
pushed a chair in front of it."

"Good girl."

She heard his vehicle start—and the line clicked. Had she lost him?

"Heath!"

"Sorry about that. My phone automatically switches over to my vehicle's hands-free app when I start it. I promise I'll stay on the line. Tell me what you hear. Is the prowler still outside?"

"I don't know. It's gotten eerily quiet the last few minutes. He was rattling the doorknob and banging against the door as if he was ramming it with his body. But now there's silence… I don't know which is worse." Straining to hear, she prayed the would-be intruder had not breached the cabin. *It's not a random intruder. You know this. It's Larry. He's angry that you took his weapon and caused Joe to get captured.*

"Help will be there soon. I have officers about two minutes away and I'm not far behind them."

A loud bang, followed by a splintering sound, rocked the cabin. Kayla screamed, no longer able to keep her fear contained.

"What's happening?" Heath demanded, panic in his voice.

"I think he broke the door open." Footsteps sounded in the hallway. "He's inside! Hurry," she whispered urgently.

The bedroom doorknob rattled and the intruder slammed against the door. "I know you're in there. I've been watching you. Saw the sheriff drop you off earlier," Larry said in a low voice.

Kayla's body trembled. She tightened her grip on the phone and wrapped her arm around her waist. He slammed against the door again. This time the chair moved slightly, jarring her. She planted her feet against the chest at the foot of the bed and straightened her legs, pushing with all her might to keep the chair in place as a barrier between her and Larry.

"I hear him. Don't say anything. Stay on the line with me. If you have your pepper spray, be prepared to use it. But try not to get trapped where he can reach you, in case it only intensifies his rage."

She nodded, even though she knew Heath couldn't see her. Her hand wrapped around the pepper spray. She flipped open the guard and slid her thumb over the trigger. *Dear Lord, please let Heath get here in time.*

Larry growled, slamming against the bedroom door with a grunt. The door splintered, a section of the frame breaking off and dropping into the chair behind her. She turned and looked over her shoulder, meeting his eye as he peered through the broken door.

"The police are on their way," she said.

"I hope it's the sheriff," he declared, glee in his voice.

An icy chill gripped her lungs, making it difficult to breathe. A siren rent the air and, moments later, a second one joined the first. Relief washed over her.

"My deputies have arrived." Heath spoke in her ear. "Stay in the bedroom until I give you the all-clear."

"I'm not done with you yet. You got my cousin arrested. And you will pay," Larry promised. Then she heard him race out the back door.

She slumped against the chair, her heartbeat drumming in her ears. Several minutes later, there was a knock on the bedroom door. "Miss Eldridge, it's Deputy Fisher. You can come out now."

Her legs ached from the exertion of trying to hold the chair against the door. She grasped the arms of the chair and pulled herself upward, grimacing.

"Ma'am, are you okay?" The door rattled as the deputy attempted to get into the room.

"I'm fine, Deputy. Just sore from sitting on the floor."

She moved the chair out of the way, hobbled to the door and opened it. At the same instant, Heath burst through the back door. Other than the time Bridget's brother Ryan had shown up to disable the bomb strapped to her while Sawyer raced to rescue Bridget from Jonathan's clutches, she'd never been so happy to see another person.

* * *

Heath's heart skipped a beat when he saw Kayla, relief rushing over him. She was safe. The only thing that stopped him from rushing to her and enveloping her in his arms was the deputy who stood between them.

"Fisher, did you see the intruder?"

"Yes, sir. He ran into the woods as I pulled in. Deputy Moore was in pursuit. I checked the perimeter and swept the cabin to ensure there wasn't another trespasser inside. Once the area was secure, I let Miss Eldridge know it was safe to come out."

"He took off when he heard the second siren," Kayla informed them, meeting Heath's eyes. "He saw you drop me off this afternoon."

Anger, disbelief and frustration coursed through him. He clinched his hands at his sides. How had Larry found them? Had he trailed Heath without his being aware? "Fisher, patrol the perimeter. Notify me if you spot anyone lurking around. I'll stay with Miss Eldridge."

"Yes, sir."

Once the deputy had stepped outside, Heath went to Kayla and pulled her into a hug. "I'm so thankful he didn't harm you."

"Yeah, me, too," she replied, her voice muffled.

Kayla stepped back and looked up at him. A

strand of hair fell across her face. He instinctively reached out and tucked it behind her ear.

She met his gaze, offering him a half smile that didn't quite erase the fear he'd seen etched in her eyes when he'd entered the room. Turning, she crossed into the main living area and sat on the couch.

"Thank you for getting here so quickly. If your deputy had been a few minutes later…" Her voice cracked, and she bit her bottom lip.

He knew what she was thinking and exactly what would've happened if Larry had gotten his hands on her.

*Thank You, Lord, for watching over her. Please let us capture Larry before he has another chance to harm her.* "Okay, you need to pack a bag. I'm taking you to Sawyer's house."

"I can't—"

"This is not a request. It's an ord—" He swallowed the word and shoved his hand through his hair. Taking a deep breath, he released it slowly. "I'm sorry. I don't have a right to order you to do anything. I just want to keep you safe. And while I understand your desire for independence, you're safer with your brother."

"I don't disagree. But Sawyer called a few hours ago. Bridget's dad had a heart attack. They've flown to Colorado to be with her family."

"I hadn't heard." Heath sat beside her. "Will Mr. Vincent be okay?"

"They think so. He will have open-heart surgery tomorrow. Bridget wanted to be there, and Sawyer needed to go to support her."

"Of course." *Now what?* Heath jumped to his feet and paced, glancing down the hall at the broken door. He could leave a deputy to stand watch outside the rest of the night, but there was no way he could secure the back door until the hardware store opened. "There's nothing else to do. Pack a bag. You're going home with me."

"I can't do that. What will people think?"

"They'll think I'm trying to keep you alive. People in this town know my integrity. Besides, we've already spent a night in the woods." He sighed.

Kayla bowed her head. Was she praying?

"Amen," she whispered and lifted her face. "You're right. My safety is more important than what others think. Besides we both know this is simply a case of the sheriff trying to protect a visitor in his county."

Her words hit like a sucker punch to the gut. Did she not realize his concern for her went far beyond that of a sheriff's concern for someone who was a temporary resident in his county? How did she not know that this was more than his own guilt for dragging her into a dangerous situation and making her the killer's target? Could he even begin to explain it to her?

Explain what? That he admired her feisty determination to remain independent and not wallow in fear or self-pity. That she had woven her way into his…heart? *No.* What he was feeling wasn't romantic. Was it? *No.* He could not allow his feelings to take a turn in that direction.

Kayla was a new friend. Nothing more. Even if he was interested—or thought that Erin had been wrong about his ability to be a good husband and a law enforcement officer at the same time—there was no way he could ever so much as allow the slightest notion of a romance with Kayla to enter his mind. She had experienced enough fear and heartache, almost losing her life at the hands of a man she'd loved, only to survive to be tracked through the wilderness by killers after Heath caused her to crash her vehicle. He could only imagine the dangers that could befall her by association if they were romantically involved.

The story of Sean Quinn's first wife's murder at the hands of a vindictive criminal entered his mind. There was no way Heath would ever consider putting Kayla in that position. And, just like when he'd dated Erin, he could not walk away from the career he'd built in law enforcement. Being sheriff was a job that he loved. Protecting others was in his DNA, like it had been in his dad's.

"Heath… Heath?" Kayla broke into his thoughts, pulling him back to the present. She stood beside him with an overnight bag in her hand.

"You've packed."

"Yes. But where were you? Your mind seemed a million miles away." She frowned.

"I'm sorry. I was… Never mind." He had to do a better job of concentrating if he expected to keep her alive. Zoning out when Larry was lurking around would get both of them killed. Heath shook the cobwebs out of his head. "I'll have my deputy secure the back door the best he can. And I'll call Mrs. Frances in the morning to let her know what happened."

Kayla nodded, a quizzical expression on her face.

He pointed to the bag in her hand. "If you're ready, we need to get going."

They stepped out the front door to discover a cluster of people in pajamas and robes standing behind the patrol cars. He should have known the sirens and lights would draw a crowd from the guest at the bed-and-breakfast.

Mrs. Frances broke away from the group and rushed toward them. "Kayla, dear, are you all right? Deputy Fisher said there was an intruder."

"I'm fine, but I'm afraid the back door is not. I'm sorry."

"Why are you apologizing, child? You didn't break it." The older woman rubbed her jaw. "Now, let me think. Where can I put you? We're all booked. But I have a rollaway cot. I could put you up in my room, I suppose."

"There's no need for that, Mrs. Frances." Heath intervened. "Until we capture the person after her, it's best for Kayla to stay where someone can protect her."

"Oh, of course." Mrs. Frances pulled Kayla into a hug. "I'll be praying they capture him soon."

Kayla headed for her vehicle and he put a hand on her arm. "I'll drive you."

"But I'll need my vehicle to go to work tomorrow."

"Do you think that's a good idea?"

"*I think* I signed a contract to work at a clinic that is shorthanded so I need to do my job."

"All the more reason to leave your vehicle here. We don't want Larry to drive past the clinic and see it. I will drive you to and from work for the time being."

She opened her mouth as if she were going to argue but then pressed her lips closed and nodded.

He escorted her to his vehicle. Once she was seated inside, he motioned Deputy Moore over. "Tell me what happened."

"I followed him and came out on the highway

on the other side of these woods just in time to see him jump into a dark SUV and speed off."

"Are you saying he had an accomplice?"

Deputy Moore shook his head. "I don't know if the SUV had been waiting on him. Or if he flagged them down and convinced them he was a hitchhiker."

That seemed a bit too coincidental to Heath. "Follow us to my house. Lights and sirens off. Make sure we don't pick up a tail."

If the person in the dark SUV was an accomplice, the situation just became even more complicated.

# FOURTEEN

"It's been three days. No one has seen Larry or his vehicle since the night he broke into my cabin. I'm sure it will be fine for me to drive myself to work today."

"Can't you humor me? I would rather err on the side of caution."

"Yes, but Bridget and Sawyer are returning this afternoon. I've agreed to stay with them, and I would like to have my things with me, including the rental car."

Heath slowed his patrol car and did a U-turn. "Just know that I'm following you to the clinic to make sure Larry isn't lurking around."

"Fair enough." Kayla smiled and turned her head to look out the window.

"You're feeling mighty proud of yourself, aren't you? For getting your way."

Pursing her lips, she tried to stop the laughter that threatened. But one look in his direction and it escaped, filling the vehicle. Tears streamed down her face. She wiped them away with the back of her hand as she fought to control herself. "I'm sorry. I don't know why I'm laughing so hard. Most likely it's just a reflex from the stress of the past few days."

Heath smiled as he pulled to a stop behind her rental car. "Do you need anything out of the cabin?"

"No. I can stop by after work to get my stuff." She opened her door, but he put out a hand to halt her. "I'll have Sawyer or Bridget meet me here, if that's what you're concerned about."

"That would be wise, but I need you to wait here. I'll check out the vehicle to make sure Larry hasn't come back and tampered with anything. Let me have your key."

"Do you think that's needed?"

Heath raised an eyebrow. "He owns an automotive shop."

"Good point." She dug into her purse and extracted the key, dropping it into his palm.

Kayla watched as he walked around the compact car she had rented, checking the tires. Next, he opened the hood and disappeared behind it. Shutting it, he dropped to the ground and lay on his stomach, searching underneath the vehicle. Then he stood and walked backward until he reached the front of his cruiser. Holding out the key fob, he pressed the remote start button. After the car idled for several minutes, he jogged to her door and opened it.

"Okay. I think it's safe for you to drive."

"Was all that completely necessary?" she asked, climbing out of the cruiser. "What were you expecting to find? A bomb?"

"It's happened before." He placed the keys in her outstretched hand. "I'm glad it wasn't the case this time."

A shiver ran up her spine. "Yeah. Me, too."

She took a step toward her vehicle. He caught her hand. Turning, she met his gaze, concern written on his face.

"I know things have been quiet the last few days, but don't let your guard down. Larry doesn't strike me as someone who will forgive and forget."

Worry lines etched his forehead. Kayla wished she could massage them away. She was sure that she'd added to his stress. The past three days he had driven her to and from work, calling her to check on her multiple times a day and stopping by to take her to lunch. The staff at the clinic were questioning if she and Heath were dating. She'd quickly informed them that wasn't the case. The sheriff was simply stepping in to help her out while her brother and sister-in-law were out of town. But Kayla had seen the looks from her coworkers—it was clear they didn't believe her. And, for a moment last evening, when they'd cooked dinner and cleaned the kitchen together afterward, she'd wished they were dating. Heath had all the qualities she'd dreamed of…once upon a time. If only she'd met him before Jonathan.

She had left Sawyer's home because she'd been afraid of falling into a state of depression and fear, but if she had stayed at Heath's any longer, the damage to her heart would have been a far greater risk to her health and well-being.

*Just get through the day. When Sawyer gets home and finds out what has transpired in his absence, he and Bridget will assign a bodyguard to protect you.* She hadn't told anyone, not even Heath, but if Larry wasn't caught by the end of the week, she planned to contact her agency to request they send a replacement to Barton Creek to take over her contract.

Fifteen minutes later, Kayla pulled into the parking lot of the medical clinic, Heath close behind. She sat in her car while he slowly circled the building. Once he completed the sweep, he parked in the space beside her, hopped out and walked over, opening her door for her.

"There is no sign of Larry or his truck." He jerked his head toward the blue Mini Cooper parked two spaces away. "Do you know who that vehicle belongs to?"

"Yes. It belongs to Dr. Lester." She looked around the otherwise empty staff parking area. "It doesn't seem anyone else has arrived yet."

"I'll walk you to the door. Make sure you lock

it and keep the building secure until opening time. If you see Larry—"

"Call your office immediately." She smiled. "I know I haven't seemed very grateful these last few days—for you babysitting me—but I appreciate all you've done to keep me alive."

"I wouldn't exactly call it babysitting." Blue eyes searched her face. "It's been nice having someone else around. Especially since you helped cook and clean. Being a bachelor, my home isn't always as tidy as it should be. Or, at least, that's what my mom tells me. But I'm sure that's typical for most males."

"I wouldn't know. You may not know my and Sawyer's story, but we didn't grow up together. My dad divorced his mother when Sawyer was two and never looked back. Dad was remorseful and tried to find Sawyer after being diagnosed with cancer. Unfortunately, he passed away before he could make amends. Mom helped me continue the search. I finally met Sawyer when I was eighteen years old."

"I'm sorry. That must have been difficult for both you and Sawyer."

She shook her head to clear the negative thoughts and forced a smile. "My point is I never knew what it was like to live with a brother. In the last few days, I feel like I've gotten a glimpse of what I missed out on."

"Don't you know when a woman tells a man

he's *like a brother to her* it hits like a dagger to his heart." He clutched his chest, smiling. "Seriously, I'm glad it hasn't been too painful for you to be guarded by me."

Had she really implied he was like a brother to her? That hadn't been what she'd meant at all. Although she really needed to consider him to be just that—an honorary brother. The past few days, there had been many times when she'd been drawn to his smile and his sky-blue eyes. While she'd been in his home, he'd been nothing but honorable, giving her as much privacy as possible. She had appreciated his thoughtfulness, but the moments she'd enjoyed most were the times they'd spent sitting on the back porch in the mornings, drinking coffee and silently reading their Bibles as the sun rose.

The first morning at his home, she'd gone in search of the perfect place to read scripture and had been surprised to find him outside in prayer. When he'd seen her, he'd instantly invited her to join him. She wasn't sure why, but she had. And that time had quickly become her favorite part of her day. She would miss it now that she was moving out. If only the scars and baggage of her past relationships didn't run as deep or fccl as heavy, she might consider him as more than an honorary brother and friend.

No. She shook her head. Kayla could not let

those thoughts take root. There was no place for them, even in the furthest recesses of her mind.

"I appreciate all you've done. I'll miss being watched by you." She clamped her mouth closed and gritted her teeth. That hadn't exactly been what she'd meant to say.

Heath arched an eyebrow and heat crept up her neck. Stepping back, he indicated she should lead the way. Closing her car door and clicking the lock button on the remote, she followed the walkway to the side door of the clinic with him close behind. She knocked and waited for admittance. No answer. Meeting Heath's gaze, she shrugged and knocked harder.

Dr. Lester opened the door, looking rather frazzled—her clothes wrinkled and her hair coming free from her normally-smooth low bun. "Oh. Kayla, you're early."

"Only a few minutes. Is everything okay?"

"Of course. I was just wrestling with…the coffee machine." She moistened her lips. "I'm not at my best until I've had my caffeine fix."

"Sally showed me how to work the machine on my first day. I can prepare you a cup." At the time, Kayla hadn't understood the office manager making sure she understood how to operate the massive coffee machine, but maybe she'd known there would come a day when Kayla would need the information.

"Yes, well…" Dr. Lester's eyes darted right and then left. Was she looking for someone?

"Is everything okay?" Kayla asked.

"Everything is fine." The doctor shrugged slightly, her eyes shifting from Kayla to the door and back again. "Just thinking about all that is happening today."

"I guess that's my cue to get out of y'all's way, so you ladies can prepare for your day." Heath squeezed Kayla's hand. "I'll pick you up at noon for lunch." He turned and hurried toward his patrol vehicle.

"Sheriff!" Dr. Lester closed her eyes and pursed her lips.

Heath stopped and turned. "Yes?"

The doctor shook her head and offered a half smile. "Have a good day. Make sure you catch the bad guys."

He raised a hand in farewell, settled into his vehicle and backed out of the parking space.

Kayla followed the doctor inside. "Are you sure you're okay? Your skin is pale and…" She reached out and placed the back of her hand on her new boss's forehead. "Your skin is clammy. Do you feel ill?"

"I'm sorry." The doctor frowned, tears welling in her eyes.

"Sorry? What are you sorry about?"

"Me." Larry spoke from behind the door.

Kayla jumped and twisted around to come

face-to-face with the man who wanted her dead. She reached for the door handle but he slammed the door shut and locked it.

"How did you get in here?" Kayla backed away from the man who'd filled her dreams with terror since their paths had first crossed.

"It wasn't hard." A female's voice sounded behind Kayla. She spun to see a petite woman, who appeared to be at the end of her pregnancy, step from behind the doctor. "We simply convinced the doctor I was experiencing a medical emergency. She kindly opened the door and let us in."

Kayla's eyes widened as she looked from the woman to Larry—a rifle in his hand—and back again. The woman rubbed her rounded belly. "I wouldn't normally get involved in something like this, but my sweet baby and I need daddy home, not in jail."

Larry reached around the woman, grasped Dr. Lester's arm and shoved her into a chair. Then pointed his weapon at Kayla. "Tie her up. And don't try any funny business. Make sure the knots are secure."

"What? Larry, no." The woman grasped his arm, a frown on her face. "You said no one was going to get hurt. We're just here to tell our story, so the lady can convince the sheriff to listen."

"You are so gullible." He shook free of her hold and pressed ropes into Kayla's hands. "If either of you don't do as I say, I'll shoot the doctor."

Kayla's throat tightened. *Dear Lord, Dr. Lester had been trying to warn us. That's why she kept moving her eyes. How did we miss the clues?*

She dropped to her knees in front of the doctor. "What time will the others arrive?" Kayla whispered under her breath, her body blocking the doctor's face from their assailant.

*Fifteen minutes,* the doctor mouthed.

Kayla tied her boss's ankles together—loose enough the cords didn't cut into her skin but tight enough Larry wouldn't become enraged if he checked her work. A cold sweat broke out along her hairline as visions of Jonathan's smirking face while he'd strapped a bomb to Kayla and tied her to a chair flashed before her eyes.

She stood on wobbly legs and moved behind the chair. Then she sighed out a breath, knelt and tied the doctor's hands together. Leaning close as she rose to her feet, Kayla whispered, "I won't let them hurt you."

"Stop talking," Larry demanded.

Kayla looked down at her feet, praying if she was submissive and not combative her boss and coworkers would be spared.

"What time will the other employees be here?" Larry asked almost the identical question Kayla had only moments before.

"They—"

"We're short-staffed today. No one else is coming," Kayla interrupted her boss, lifting her head to meet the killer's eyes. *Lord, forgive my lie.* "The other nurse is on a leave of absence. It's just me and the doctor today."

"What about the receptionist? Someone has to greet the patients." Larry persisted.

"She won't be here for almost an hour. Typically walks in the door right at opening time."

"If you just started, how would you know that?"

"How do you know I just started?"

The man shrugged. "A hunch. Your car had out-of-state plates, and your trunk was full of clothes and things."

"You're right. I'm a temporary—traveling—nurse." Kayla squared her shoulders and prayed he would believe her. "You don't think the person I'm filling in for would have told me the ins-and-outs of the running of the office?" She looked at the doctor and winked, hoping Dr. Lester would realize it was all an act.

"Please don't hurt anyone, Larry," the petite pregnant woman begged. "Let's just go. We'll think of another way to get Joe out of jail. I can come up with the bond somehow. The longer we wait around, the greater the risk the sheriff will return."

"Let him." Larry raised his rifle and pointed it at the door. "I should've killed him when I had the chance a few moments ago."

The woman slapped Larry's arm. "No, you

shouldn't have. If you had killed him, we would be on the run now. And you promised me we were going to get Joe out of jail."

"We will. Just as soon as I can arrange the swap."

*Swap?* Larry was taking her hostage again. She suspected the word swap had only been used for the pregnant woman's benefit. Kayla knew without a doubt Larry would only allow her to live long enough to gain Joe's release.

"I'll promise you another thing, too." He looked through the scope and slowly swung the gun around until it was pointed at Kayla. "When this is over, I'm going hunting."

Fear gripped her at his confirmation of her suspicions. An involuntary shiver shook her body.

Larry laughed. "Bang."

# FIFTEEN

Heath's desk phone rang. He snatched the receiver. "Sheriff Dalton."

"Sheriff, thought you might want to know we found Larry Frye's truck," Deputy Moore said.

"Where?" Heath jumped to his feet, rounded his desk and headed for the door, pulling the phone off the desktop. For a moment, he'd forgotten he wasn't on his cell.

"The hardware store parking lot. We're canvassing the area, looking for him now."

His chest tightened. The hardware store was less than half a mile from the medical clinic. "I'm on my way."

Placing the phone back on the desk, he returned the handset to the cradle. He ran out of his office as his landline rang again. His footsteps faltered. Should he answer it? No. Whatever it was couldn't be as important as his need to get to the scene and find Larry.

Heath pulled his cell phone out of his pocket and dialed Kayla's number. The clinic would open in ten minutes. She needed to keep the doors locked until he could get a deputy over there to stand guard.

"Sheriff!" The dispatch supervisor raced down the hall toward him, her gray hair flying out behind her, her face flushed. "Sheriff!"

"If it's not important, it'll have to wait." Heath continued toward the exit. He didn't have time to discuss the pay raise Carol had been hounding him about.

*Third ring. Why isn't Kayla picking up?*

"Sheriff." Carol ran in front of him and stopped, blocking the door. "Dr. Lester is on the phone with Dispatch. Kayla Eldridge has been abducted."

"What! Why am I just hearing this?"

"We called, but you didn't answer. I was about to try your cell phone, but then I saw you and… thought this was faster." Carol took several deep breaths.

"You have fifteen seconds to fill me in on the details as we *quickly* walk to my vehicle," Heath commanded, reaching around her and opening the door.

"Larry Frye and a pregnant female accomplice took Kayla twenty minutes ago."

"Twenty minutes! Why are we just now being notified?" In a situation like this, every minute wasted could be the difference in life or death.

"They tied Dr. Lester to a chair. She had to

wait until another employee arrived and untied her to call it in."

"And no one saw which direction they went?"

"The doctor didn't. I don't know if anyone else in the area did. We have deputies en route to the clinic."

They reached his patrol car. Heath placed a hand on the door handle. "If anyone calls with new information, patch them through to me. Got it?"

"Yes, sir."

He jumped into his vehicle and sped out of the parking lot, lights activated and siren blaring. The next time he saw his friend Sean Quinn, he would apologize to him. Heath had not completely understood the urgency and fear Sean had experienced five months ago when his wife Jenna had been the one in danger. But he did now.

"Lord, I know my prayers this week have been full of requests and not so much my thanks for my many blessings. I do not take any of my blessings for granted, and I thank You with my whole heart for all that You have given me. But, Lord, could I please have one more blessing? I don't know how Kayla did it, but she warmed her way into my heart. Lord, I need her to stay alive. Please don't let Larry and his accomplice hurt her. Because my heart would break completely in half if something were to happen to her."

He knew they could never be more than

friends—and she would move to her next assignment soon—but knowing she was alive and well somewhere in this world would be enough.

Turning into the medical clinic's staff parking area, he parked in the exact spot he'd vacated earlier, beside Kayla's rental. Deputy Fisher greeted him as Heath exited his vehicle. Heath looked toward the main parking lot where Deputy Bishop and the clinic's receptionist stood together near the entrance. A small black sedan driven by an elderly man pulled in. The driver rolled down his window, and the receptionist consulted the clipboard she held in her hands. "What are they doing?"

"They're giving patients the option of rescheduling their appointments or parking and remaining in their vehicles until they're allowed inside to be treated."

The sedan pulled forward and parked beside two other cars with people who had chosen to wait.

"Then I guess we need to get the questioning over with so these people can get on with their day." Taking long strides, he walked up the same sidewalk he'd crossed less than an hour earlier. Images of the doctor's eyes moving from side to side and her comment telling him to *catch the bad guys* flashed through his brain. The clues had been right in front of him. She'd been trying to tell him *the bad guys* were inside the clinic.

Larry had been steps away from him and Heath had let him slip away once again.

"Larry is probably long gone from the area. Call all the surrounding police departments and see if any of them can put up checkpoints on the main roads." Heath knew it would probably be a futile exercise, but he had to feel like he was doing something.

Thirty minutes later, after getting a full statement from the doctor and the nurse who had found her tied to the chair, he granted permission for the clinic to open and walked out of the building.

His phone rang as he reached his patrol vehicle. Pulling the phone out of his back pocket, he prayed it was Carol with news of an eyewitness. Kayla's number flashed on the screen. His heart skipped a beat. "Kayla, where are you? Did you escape?"

Laughter echoed across the line. "Looks like someone spoiled my surprise," Larry drawled.

"Where is she, Larry? You better not have hurt her."

"Whether she lives or dies is up to you, Sheriff. You have something I want. I have something you want. Maybe we could work out a trade that benefits both of us?"

Anger, mingled with fear that Kayla was in the hands of this killer, coursed through him. He clenched his teeth, his jaw twitching. "Tell me your demands."

"You release Joe. I'll consider releasing your lady."

"Do you think I have the power to let him go? Burying a body in a national park is a federal offense. It's out of my hands."

"Okay, then I'm finished with this conversation. The lady's death will be on your head."

Kayla, gasping in pain, sounded in the background.

"No. Wait! I'll make it happen. I'll meet you to trade." He tightened his grip on the phone. The necessity of the occasional lie had never sat well with Heath, but he had to buy time to work out the details and develop a plan to get Kayla back. "Joe is scheduled to go before the judge in an hour. I'll come up with a reason why I'm the only one that can drive him. Then I'll meet you with him after we leave the courthouse."

"I'm not waiting that long."

"Look I'm not naïve enough to think that you're going to let me walk away after I release Joe. But even a criminal can be a man of his word. I'm holding you to your promise to let Kayla go if I bring your cousin to you. She's an innocent bystander that got caught in the tangled situation we find ourselves in because of me. Letting her go won't cost you anything. She doesn't have the power to hurt you."

A female voice he didn't recognize spoke in hushed tones in the background. There was a moment's pause, then Larry came back on the line. "Okay. You bring Joe, and the woman will walk free. But we're not waiting an hour to do the exchange."

*Think fast, Dalton!* "If Joe disappears and doesn't show up at the preliminary hearing, there will be an all-out manhunt for me and him. And you. If I drive him to the hearing and we take a detour on our way back to the jail to meet you, it will be a couple of hours before we're missed."

"You're just trying to stall so you can set a trap."

"Look, you said Kayla's life is in my hands. Do you really think I would do anything to put her in jeopardy?" He puffed out a breath. "If anyone figures out what's going on, they'll come after me—it's a federal offense to help a criminal escape. They won't care that I'm the sheriff. If that happens, Kayla *and* the pregnant lady you have helping you will be caught in the crossfire. Is that what you want? For your lady friend and her unborn child to lose their lives? I promise you, I don't want Kayla to lose hers because of me."

There was another exchange of words between Larry and the unknown woman "Okay. But don't think about tracing the location of this call, because this phone is about to go in the river. I'll be somewhere far away in an hour."

"If you throw the phone away, how am I going to know where to bring Joe?"

"A preliminary hearing shouldn't last over thirty minutes—"

"Actually, it can take up to two hours."

"You better hope it doesn't," Larry roared. "I'm calling you in ninety minutes. If you don't answer, the woman dies. And I disappear."

"Let me talk—"

The line went dead.

"No!"

Kayla sat on the floorboard in the back seat of the newer model SUV Larry drove, with her hands tied together. He must have ditched the old rusty truck Heath had told her he'd been seen driving.

The pregnant woman, who sat in the front with Larry, glanced over the seat at Kayla. "Don't you think she can sit in the seat now? We're out of the city limits. This road doesn't look like it's very well traveled."

"No. It's better if she stays out of sight. I'm sure the sheriff has put out an alert. If a police officer gets a glimpse of her, they'll pull me over."

"Do you seriously think they could see into the back seat as you drove by? The tint on the windows is so dark it's impossible to see inside unless you have your face plastered against the glass."

"This is all your husband's fault, anyway. If he hadn't shot Ray, we wouldn't be in this mess."

"Stop saying that. There's no way Joe murdered anyone. My husband is a good, church-going, God-fearing man. If he's caught up in something crooked, it's all you're doing." She glanced back at Kayla once again. "Go ahead, climb up in the seat. He ain't going to shoot you. Just sit still, and don't make him angry."

Kayla cautiously followed the instructions, choosing to settle on the seat directly behind Larry. Hopefully, he would have a more difficult time grabbing hold of her if he reached for her.

"Thank you," she said to the woman.

Larry grunted but didn't order her to get back on the floor.

As they traveled further and further away from Barton Creek, Kayla observed the woman. She appeared to be about the same age as Kayla. Her strawberry-blond hair had been pulled back in a ponytail, and her face was makeup free, displaying a sprinkling of freckles spattered across her nose and cheeks. "When is your baby due?"

"Next month." The woman smiled, but it didn't quite reach her blue eyes, which looked as if they may have experienced as much heartache and pain as Kayla had.

"Is this your first?"

A frown marred her youthful-looking face. "Yeah."

She had seen that same expression of great loss on the faces of many women in the exam room through the years. Kayla may be a terrible judge of men, but she understood women. It was obvious to her this woman was not a bad person. Most likely, she had been dragged into this situation the same as Kayla. "Do you know what you're having?"

"It's a baby girl. Lila Rose. Joe and I have been praying for a baby for several years." She rubbed her stomach. "God has finally blessed us."

"Shut up, Brenda. No one wants to hear that nonsense. God didn't *give* you a baby. You and Joe, along with an army of doctors and nurses and the latest medicine, are the only reason that baby exists."

Tears welled in Brenda's eyes, her lower lip quivering. She crossed her arms over her rounded belly and turned to look out the side window.

There was little doubt in Kayla's mind that this woman hadn't willingly gone along with the plan to abduct her. If she wasn't pregnant, Kayla would use that to her advantage and gain her help in escaping. But there was no way Kayla could put the woman or her innocent unborn child at risk of being harmed.

The trio rode in silence as Larry drove deeper and deeper into the mountains. Where was he taking them? He still had her phone, but he'd told Heath he was tossing it into the river. Had that been a lie? No, he wouldn't have lied about that. Keeping the phone would give Heath an advantage tracking them. They reached a narrow one-lane bridge, and Larry rolled down his window and tossed her phone into the water below as he sped across it, confirming her theory.

*Lord, please let Heath save me.*

She didn't know what the sheriff's plan was, but she knew him well enough to know his position as sheriff meant more to him than anything else in this world. Larry might be fooled into thinking Heath would go along with the demand to release Joe, but Kayla knew better. There was no way he'd turn a killer loose, no matter whose life was in danger if he didn't. However, she knew he would do everything in his power to save her.

Larry turned onto a narrow, rundown road that wove up the mountain.

"Where are we going?" Brenda sat straighter. "You said you would take me home. That I just needed to ride with you so that you could get inside the clinic to speak to the woman that could convince the sheriff Joe was innocent. I never would have come with you if I'd known you were going to kidnap her. You've made me an accomplice." She burst into tears. "I can't go to jail!"

"Shut up!" he bellowed. "Don't you realize by now the kind of situation we're in? No matter how much *you* want to deny it, Ray's death was not an accident. He discovered we were running drugs out of the auto shop. And—"

"Drugs? You're dealing drugs? What have you gotten us involved in, Larry?"

"Oh, come on, little sister. Don't act so shocked. Besides, it's not like I'm peddling them on the elementary school playground. All I'm doing is transporting them."

*Sister? So, Larry and Joe were brothers-in-law, and that's how Larry had manipulated Brenda.*

"But drugs? How could you get mixed up in something like that? You need to turn around now. We need to go back, so you can come clean to the sheriff." She grabbed his arm, pulling and tugging as she fought to get him to stop the vehicle.

He jerked his arm free of her hold and back-handed Brenda across the face, knocking her against the passenger's-side window. Kayla lunged forward.

"Don't think about it." He pinned her with a look that clearly stated he would not hesitate to stop the vehicle, put a bullet through her head and be done with her. She sank back against the seat.

"And you…" He glared at Brenda. "Don't tell me what I should and shouldn't do. How do you think we paid for the fertility treatments? They're not cheap, and we're not rich. But you wanted a baby, so Joe and I did what we had to do to make it happen."

Brenda stayed slumped against her door with her arms wrapped protectively around her belly, her shoulders shaking as sobs racked her body. Kayla's heart ached for the other woman. In that moment, she knew it would be up to her to get both her and Brenda away from Larry. She would not wait to be rescued.

Four years ago, she hadn't fought back soon enough and had ended up in a chair with dynamite strapped to her. Not this time. She didn't know how she'd prevent Larry from killing her, but she wouldn't go down without a fight.

# SIXTEEN

Heath glanced at the clock on his office wall. *Time is running out!*

"Does everyone understand their assignment?" He looked at the officers gathered in his office. His eyes landed on Deputy Fisher—five years younger and two inches taller than Joe but with the same basic build and wavy brown hair. For once, Heath was glad the youthful deputy had skipped a few haircuts—his hair brushed his collar, just like Joe's. "Fisher?"

"Yes, sir. I will wear handcuffs, keep my face turned toward the ground at all times, and do my absolute best to act like the prisoner." He looked at the orange inmate outfit he wore. "When we get close enough the suspect can see us, but not close enough for him to identify me, you will unlock my handcuffs. And my weapon will be here." He lifted the hem of the loose-fitting shirt to reveal his department-issued weapon tucked inside a holster.

"Good." Heath turned to the two officers

dressed in casual wear. "Deputy Bishop, what is your assignment?"

"Deputy McNeal and I will be undercover as a husband and wife. We will be trailing you in an unmarked car, stopping periodically at roadside stands in case Larry has accomplices stationed along the route watching. As I'm driving, Deputy McNeal will search for additional routes to the location so we can deploy officers and attempt a sneak attack."

Finally, Heath gave his attention to his chief deputy. "Officers from the surrounding area are on standby?"

"Yes, sir," Deputy Moore replied. "Each department is providing assistance. I have informed them of your wishes they conduct all communication by cell phone to prevent civilians—especially Larry—from listening in on a police scanner. I've also apprised Agent Knight of the situation."

"Okay, sounds like everyone knows the plan. Nothing to do now but wait for Larry's phone call." Heath looked at the clock. "It's five minutes past the time he said he would call."

"Is there anything you need us to do in the meantime, sir?" Deputy Moore inquired.

"I want everyone in their vehicles. Be ready to roll as soon as I get the call."

After the other officers left, Heath walked over to Deputy Fisher and fastened handcuffs on his officer's hands. "It's very important that you play the part, even when you don't think anyone is watching. We don't know where Larry is or if he has other accomplices."

When they reached his patrol vehicle, Heath opened the door and helped Deputy Fisher settle into the back. Then he ducked inside the vehicle, removed the handcuffs and dropped them onto his officer's lap. "Slip these back on when we get close."

"Yes, sir." Fisher bowed his head with a smile.

Heath closed the door, jogged around the vehicle and slid behind the wheel. Starting the engine, he backed out of his assigned parking space.

"Where are we headed, sir?" Deputy Fisher asked.

Heath tapped his thumb on the steering wheel. "I'm not sure. I just needed out of the office and wanted to be in position, so when I get the call, I'll be that much closer to reaching Kayla."

"I understand, sir."

Glancing up, he locked eyes with his deputy's reflection in the review mirror. What exactly did Fisher understand? Heath wished he could ask, because he himself did not understand why he felt antsy about what was happening. In his thirteen years in law enforcement, he'd been involved in many high-stake cases. In all of them, he'd remained calm and collected. This time, he felt as if his heart was going to beat out of his chest. If he didn't get to Kayla in time…

He could not let his mind go there. *Lord, please keep her safe. I love her, and—* Love? Yes, love. Heath loved Kayla. Even though he'd not admitted it to himself, he'd subconsciously known his true feelings for several days. And if he'd read his deputy's thoughts correctly, it seemed like the people around him had also figured it out.

Heath's phone rang and he jumped. Agent Knight's name flashed on the screen on his dashboard. He parked in an empty space close to the parking lot exit and tapped the answer button on the screen with his finger. "This is Sheriff Dalton."

"Sheriff, I have agents stationed throughout the park on lookout in case Larry returns to our area. I've also dispatched an officer to your office with instructions to ride along with one of your deputies."

"Sorry, can't allow that. I won't put Kayla's life in jeopardy. If Larry see—"

"Sheriff, you know this is a federal case. As such, the FBI has every right to be included in the takedown."

"And get Kayla killed in the process." Heath seethed as anger radiated throughout his body.

"No one wants that," Agent Knight said. "However, I'd like to point out I've cooperated with you. It's your turn to cooperate with me.

My man should arrive at your office any minute now."

As if to punctuate the agent's words, a dark SUV pulled into the parking lot.

Heath silently exhaled a breath. "I'll accommodate your request. But tell your agent as long as we're in my jurisdiction, they're to stand back and wait for my orders."

A beep sounded. He glanced at the phone screen. An unknown number. It had to be Larry.

"I have to take this. I'll call you back." Heath ended the call and accepted the new one. "This is Sheriff Dalton. How may I help you?"

"My, you sound so formal, Sheriff. Here I thought we were becoming friends," Larry chuckled.

"We'll discuss our friendship *after* you release Kayla." Heath gritted his teeth and his jaw twitched.

"Does that mean you have Joe? Let me talk to him."

"No deal. You didn't let me speak to Kayla, so you don't get to speak to Joe."

"Fine. You can talk to your girl."

A scraping sound, like a chair being pushed on a tiled floor, came over the line, followed by Larry muttering something in the background.

"Heath." Kayla's frightened voice filled Heat's vehicle. His breath caught. "Don't do it. Don't let a killer out of jail—Oww!"

"Kayla! Kayla, don't antagonize him. Do what he says. I'll be there soon." More scraping and scuffling noises sounded. A helpless feeling washed over him and his hands tightened on the steering wheel. "Larry! Larry, you better not hurt her."

A few seconds later, Larry returned, breathing heavily. "You heard her voice. Let me talk to Joe."

"Did you hurt her? If you did, I will hunt you down. There will be no place you can hide from me."

"Take it easy, Sheriff. The girl's okay. She just needs to learn to keep her mouth shut. And I'm not telling you again. I either talk to Joe or I kill the girl. You try to come find me, I'll kill you, too."

Heath muted the call, twisted in his seat and looked over his shoulder at Deputy Fisher. "Are you ready?"

"Yes." Fisher nodded.

The young officer had spent an hour listening to the recordings of Joe's interrogation and had created multiple small sound bites that would be appropriate for casual conversation. Hopefully, they could use the sound bites to convince Larry that Joe was in the vehicle.

"Sheriff, what's taking so long? Let me talk to Joe now," Larry demanded. "If you don't, I'm hanging up the phone."

Heath unmuted the phone and silently released

a slow breath. "Okay, he's here. I'll let you speak to him."

"Hey, Larry."

"Joe, is that really you?"

The deputy clicked on another audio clip. "Who did you expect?"

Larry laughed. "We're gonna get you home. Brenda ain't gonna have this baby alone."

Heath looked at Fisher and raised an eyebrow. The pregnant woman with Larry was Joe's wife. The deputy frowned.

"Joe. You still there?"

"Yeah." Fisher selected another clip. "Don't hurt the girl."

"You let me worry about how to handle things from here on out. You've created enough troubles."

"This ain't on me," Joe's gruff voice replied. Heath was amazed at the various responses Deputy Fisher had prepared. This was going better than he'd hoped for.

There was a muffled conversation between Larry and the woman.

"Sheriff, Brenda wants to talk to Joe."

Heath hadn't planned on a conversation between the computerized Joe and Brenda. Would she ask something they couldn't answer and blow their cover?

"No. Enough of this," Heath said emphatically. "I can't keep sitting here waiting to meet you. I told you I have a short window of time to make the swap before someone gets suspicious and officers start searching for us."

"I understand, Sheriff," a woman's voice replied meekly. "I'm sorry for…everything. Joe's really not a bad guy. I wanted him to know I understood none of this was his fault. He let my brother guide him dow—"

"Give me that phone!" Larry growled. "Sheriff, I'm texting the address. If I see anyone other than you and Joe, I'll kill everyone. Your girl and Brenda included. I don't want to leave all these dead bodies behind. The choice is yours. Don't try to double-cross me. You have exactly forty-five minutes to get here or we'll be gone."

The line went dead and, immediately, Heath's phone dinged. They had the address. Now, he only had to figure out how to execute the plan without risk to the woman he loved *and* a killer's wife and her unborn child.

Kayla fisted her hands and struggled against the rope, desperate to loosen its hold on her wrists. Her heart thundered in her chest, and she broke out in a cold sweat. *Lord, why are You allowing me to be tortured like this?*

It wasn't the Lord's fault. It was hers. If she hadn't accepted the position in Barton Creek, she wouldn't have been driving through the national park when Heath ran out into the road. *Heath.* If his wounds had gone untreated, the infection and fever would have gotten worse. Would he have made it out of the woods? Her throat tightened. Kayla gasped. She couldn't catch her breath.

*Breathe in...two...three...four...*
*Hold...two...three...four...*
*Release...two...three...four...*

Brenda paced the floor, as she had for the past thirty minutes, while rubbing her lower back. After Larry had tied Kayla to the chair, he'd demanded his sister "stand watch over the prisoner." Then he had stormed outside with his gun and a pair of binoculars to make sure "that Sheriff didn't break his promise and bring an army of deputies with him."

Could she convince Brenda to untie her?

"I don't want to get you in trouble with Larry. But my shoulder hurts and my hands are numb..." Kayla pleaded with her eyes for compassion from the other woman. "If you untie me—actually, if you would just loosen the rope a small amount, it would help. Please."

Brenda paused in midstride and looked at Kayla, tears in her eyes. "I'm so sorry... If I had known... I never would have..." She closed her eyes and blew out a breath. "I feel like I've stepped into some strange, alternate science-fiction universe."

She opened her eyes and pinned Kayla with a helpless look. "I don't even recognize my brother…his behavior…the things he's said Joe has done. How could I have missed seeing the truth all these years?"

"Unfortunately, I probably understand what you're going through better than anyone else you will ever meet."

"Oh, really? Were you pregnant and discovered that your husband had been operating an illegal drug business and ended up on the run from the law?"

Kayla held Brenda's gaze, refusing to blink. "Have you ever heard of the serial killer Lovelorn?"

Brenda whitened and her mouth formed an *O*. "Were you married to him?"

"Engaged. He used me because he had a vendetta against my brother, an FBI profiler who had saved one of Jonathan's targets from becoming one of his victims." Kayla's voice cracked. "I thought Jonathan was taking me to meet his parents, to let them know we were getting married. Instead, he took me to a cabin in the woods—much like this one—tied me to a chair…" She huffed. "Strapped a bomb to me and left me… For three days, I sat—unable to move—waiting for the bomb to go *boom*."

Brenda sank onto the sofa, as if every muscle in her body had stopped working.

"Thankfully, my brother and his friends arrived in time to save me. But just barely. The bomb actually detonated less than three minutes after we raced out of the cabin." Kayla looked down at her feet. "As you can imagine, being tied to this chair right now, in a cabin, in the woods, is bringing back a lot of horrific memories." It was taking every ounce of willpower for her not to burst into tears.

Brenda pressed her hand down on the couch arm and pushed herself upward. Then she waddled over to Kayla, pulled a dining table chair closer, sat and untied the rope holding Kayla's arms behind her. "I can't bend over to untie your feet. Sorry."

"That's fine." Kayla rubbed her wrists, thankful for the other woman's compassion. Then she bent over and untied her ankles. "What about Larry? I don't want him to take his anger out on you for removing the ropes."

"Just tell him I did it because I'm in labor."

"You will have to really put on a good act." Kayla smiled.

"No, actually, I don't think I will. Because... Oooh..." The other woman wrapped her arms around her rounded belly and doubled over, taking shallow breaths and puffing air out in short bursts. "That one was strong."

"Brenda, you're in labor!" Kayla rushed to her side.

"I told you." She rubbed her stomach. "If I

wasn't about to cry, I might laugh, but right now this doesn't feel very funny."

Kayla guided Brenda down the short hall to the bedroom. She eased Kayla onto the bed. "Did you take birthing classes?"

Brenda nodded.

"Okay, I want you to concentrate on your breathing." Kayla demonstrated. "Hee…hee… hoo…"

Picking up Brenda's wrist, Kayla placed the tip of her index and third fingers over the radial artery, silently counting the heartbeats. Brenda's pulse was high, but within the expected range for a woman in labor. Kayla wished she had her blood pressure cuff and scope. If Brenda's blood pressure soared, both she and the baby would be in danger. "When did the contractions start?"

"My back started hurting while we were at the clinic this morning. I thought it was just normal pregnancy aches. Then, in the car, right before we got here, I started having some pains. I wrote them off as Braxton-Hicks contractions. I'm only thirty-six weeks. It's too soon!" Panic rose in Brenda's voice.

A door slammed and footsteps sounded in the living room. "Brenda, where are you? Where's the prisoner?" Larry bellowed.

Kayla raced to the bedroom door, closed and locked it, and pushed the dresser in front of it.

Once again, she found herself in a showdown against Larry, with her being trapped in a bedroom.

"Open. The. Door."

"Larry," Kayla said in her calming nurse voice, "Brenda is in labor. I can't have you upsetting her."

"You're lying! The baby isn't due until next month." He banged on the door. "Open this door, or I'll shoot through it."

"If you do that, you risk hitting your sister and killing her and your niece."

"Listen to her, Larry. Go away."

"Brenda! Open this door!" He slammed against the door, trying to fight his way in.

"Can't. I'm in labor, dummy." Brenda took several short breaths.

"Let me in! Ugh!" Larry repeatedly slammed against the door.

"Larry, I'm not opening the door. It will stay barricaded. I need to protect myself and my patient."

"That's my sister in there. Let me in."

"No, sir. But I promise I'm not going to try to escape. I will not leave Brenda's side while she's in labor."

"If you do, I will take great pleasure in tracking you down and killing you in the most torturous manner possible."

Kayla's body trembled uncontrollably. She

wrapped her arms around her middle, holding as tightly as she could. *Dear Lord, let Heath get here soon. Let him save me, Brenda and her baby.* She crossed to her patient and put an extra pillow under her head. "You're doing great. Don't think about Larry or everything else that's going on right now. Concentrate on this new life you're bringing into the world."

Brenda looked up, tears streaming down her face. "Kayla, you need to sneak out the window and run. Run as fast as you can. I know Larry. He's not going to let you leave here with your life."

"I can't do that. You need me, and Lila Rose needs me. I won't leave you."

Kayla prayed her decision to stay wouldn't cost her her life. But she knew if she ran and something happened to Brenda or her baby, she'd never be able to live with herself.

Heath's cell phone rang and Deputy Moore's number flashed on the screen. He answered the call. "Tell me what you found."

"The cabin is not inside the national park, but it borders the national park property. Agent Knight said that he can access it from behind. He and his agents are en route, on ATVs. They plan to park the ATVs a mile from the cabin and hike the remaining distance so Larry doesn't hear them."

"According to my GPS, my ETA is ten minutes. How far behind are the agents?"

"Agent Knight said he could reach you in fifteen minutes," Moore replied.

"Every minute counts. I can't wait on him. We'll have to go in before he gets there." Heath heaved out a breath. "The road leading to this cabin doesn't appear to be well traveled. It's very curvy, and I can see the roofline of a cabin at the top of the mountain. I'm sure that's where they are, giving Larry a clear view of all incoming traffic. Tell Deputy Bishop to find a place to pull off and park for five minutes, long enough for Larry not to suspect he's following me."

Heath disconnected the call and focused on the road ahead.

"Sir, I don't want to question your authority, or any of your decisions, but is it wise to go in before backup arrives?" Fisher queried from the back seat.

"Probably not, but I don't see that we have another option. If Larry thinks that I have officers following me, he'll kill Kayla before I can reach him. And I can't risk her life."

The thought of Kayla dying coiled around his chest like a boa constrictor, almost suffocating him. Never being able to share a pizza or explore the many tourist destinations with her again would be crippling. *Dear Lord, I'm in love with her. And I don't want go through life without her by my side.* The thought made him elated and terrified at the same moment. *But You already knew that. Please, don't let me lose her now that I've found her. I don't deserve her. But if we get out of this alive—and she is open to pursuing a relationship with me—I will resign from my job and find a new, safer career. Then I will spend the rest of my life ensuring she knows how much she is loved.*

"Sir, let me take the lead. Go in first. He won't shoot me. He thinks I'm Joe."

"I can't allow you to do that. The instant he realizes you're not Joe, he will put a bullet through you."

"That's what Kevlar vests are for."

"A bulletproof vest won't help you if he decides to shoot you in the head."

"I can keep my distance and play some of the sound bites that are on my phone when he asks questions. It will give the others time to arrive."

Heath shook his head. "I'm not going to hide behind you. I'll walk in beside you, holding your nondominant arm so you can use your gun if needed."

The deputy's phone dinged and a smile spread across his face. "Deputy McNeal sent me new audio clips."

"Where's Brenda?" Joe's voice filled the vehicle. "Brenda, I'm sorry."

"There are five more, all mentioning Brenda."

"How'd she get those?" Heath spared a quick glance over his shoulder.

Fisher quickly typed a message to Deputy McNeal. His phone dinged in response almost immediately. "When she found out Brenda was involved, she called the jail and talked to Joe. She questioned him about his wife and marriage."

The deputy's phone dinged again. "When Joe found out Larry has Brenda at a cabin and is holding her and Kayla Eldridge at gunpoint, he broke down in tears and started giving details about the drug trafficking he and Larry are mixed up in. Joe said Brenda doesn't know anything about the illegal activities they're involved in." Fisher looked up and met Heath's eyes in the rearview mirror. "Joe said if we save Brenda and their baby, he'll testify in court, giving names of the people in charge of the trafficking ring."

Heath's officers' ability to get the job done never ceased to amaze him. They always stepped up and did what needed to be done to protect the citizens they were responsible for.

"Your destination is in one mile, on the right." The automated voice of the maps app alerted they were nearing the cabin.

Heath heard his deputy lock the handcuffs into place.

*Time to face a killer.* And, hopefully, outsmart him, while keeping everyone alive.

# SEVENTEEN

Heath spotted Larry the instant he turned into the drive that wound upward to a house on a hill. The killer stood on the small porch with his elbows balanced on the railing—his rifle pointed at Heath's patrol vehicle—wearing camouflage, as he had the first time Heath had seen him. "He's watching. Make sure you stay in character."

"Who you bossing around?" Fisher replied.

"Wow, you almost sounded just like Joe."

"I've been practicing. My voice isn't as deep as his." The deputy shrugged. "If the sound bites don't work, I'll wing it and try to explain the difference away as a sore throat."

Heath pulled into the circle driveway and stopped in front of the cabin, parking so his door was farthest away from the killer. "Are you ready for your acting debut?"

"Yes, sir," Fisher replied. "And I apologize ahead of time for anything I have to do today. It's not personal."

Heath gave a curt nod, opened his door and

stepped out. "Okay, Larry, we're here. But I don't see Kayla. Where is she?"

"Don't worry about her. She's inside. And she's alive. Now, let me see Joe."

"My windows are not darkened, you can see him just fine."

Larry lifted the rifle and pointed it at Heath. "Get him out, Sheriff. We're not playing games here."

Heath closed his door. Then he moved to the back one, opened it and pulled Fisher from the vehicle. Slamming the door behind them, he tugged Fisher toward the rear of the vehicle where Larry could see the handcuffed imposter.

Larry was about thirty yards away. *Please, Lord, let this work.*

Deputy Fisher turned to Heath, held out his hands and shook the handcuffs, as if demanding their removal. Heath took out the key and unlocked the cuffs, removing them from Fisher's wrists. His deputy rubbed his wrists, as if they had been bound for a long time. Then he moved to go around him and Heath grabbed his arm by the elbow. Fisher stepped back, tugged and tried to jerk free.

"What are you doing, Sheriff? Let him go. That's the deal," Larry yelled from the porch.

Heath pulled out his gun and pointed it at the fake Joe. *Forgive me, Lord, for pointing a weapon at an innocent person.* "The deal was that you would let Kayla go. I don't see her. Until I do, I don't let Joe go."

"She's detained at the moment." Larry crossed to the steps leading off the porch. "Brenda decided to go into labor. The nurse is helping her."

Heath and Fisher looked at each other. The deputy's eyes widened and he struggled, attempting to pull free. The deputy's acting was impressive.

Heath held firm, opening the door to the back seat once more and dragging him toward it. "I'll put Joe back in the car. We'll wait until the delivery is over for the exchange."

"You're going to deny a man the right to see his child being born?" Larry demanded.

Heath locked eyes with the killer. "I truly hate for him to miss something that important, but I'm not letting my bargaining chip go until Kayla is off this mountain."

The vehicle blocked Fisher's hands. He slipped his phone out of his pocket, selected a sound bite, and hit Play. "Take care of Brenda."

"What's stopping me from dropping you right now, Sheriff? I have a clear shot." Larry leaned against the porch post.

"Nothing, I guess, except you risk hitting Joe here."

"No! I want to see my baby," Joe's voice declared.

The ability of his deputy to navigate quickly

between the recordings and find the correct response astonished Heath. He shoved the deputy into the back seat—as if he were a real criminal. Then he crouched low, so Larry wouldn't have a clear shot, and pretended to slip the cuffs back onto Deputy Fisher's hands.

"Be ready to act if he shoots," Heath whispered.

"Roger that," Fisher replied under his breath and slipped his weapon out of its holster.

"Do not move until I give the order," Heath murmured and duck-walked to the rear bumper.

"Once Kayla goes free," Heath yelled, "I let my buddy Joe out of the back seat. If she can't leave because Brenda is in labor, then you need to allow me to get an ambulance up here. They can take Kayla and Brenda to the hospital, where she and the baby can get the care they need for a safe delivery."

"I told you, you had to come alone."

"And I did, but let's get the women out of here. Then it will just be the three of us guys—you, me and Joe." He peeked around the bumper.

Larry scratched his head. "I don't know. You might try to sneak some more police officers in here."

"You can listen as I radio in the request. Unless I specifically request police officers, only the ambulance will arrive on the scene. What do you say?"

Without a word, Larry ran into the house and slammed the door.

Deputy Fisher leaned out of the vehicle. Heath waved him back inside. "Stay there. Until we suspect he's not buying our act."

Fisher looked as if he was going to argue but nodded and settled back inside the vehicle.

Heath stood, hunched over slightly, and rounded his SUV. A gunshot rang out from the front window of the cabin, hitting the back fender. Heath returned fire, dove to the ground and scooted behind his vehicle once more.

He looked around the back of the SUV and caught sight of a man wearing a green FBI bulletproof vest. The agent motioned to the other side of the house. Heath ran the length of the vehicle and peered around the front. Agent Knight was looking around the opposite corner of the house. *Thank You, Lord, help has arrived.*

Fisher eased out of the back seat and closed the door softly. "I'm ready for orders."

Knowing the agents would have their phones on silent, Heath pulled out his cell, called Agent Knight and turned to watch as he answered. "Sheriff, I have two agents at the back door ready to go in."

"We have a situation. Larry is refusing to let Kayla out. His sister—Joe Granger's wife—is in the cabin and she's in labor."

\* \* \*

Gunshots, followed by the front door slamming, spurred Kayla into action. She helped Brenda to her feet, draped the quilt around her and grabbed pillows. "Let's move you to the bathtub. It may be safer since it's an interior room."

"What's going on?" Sweat glistened on Brenda's face.

"I think the sheriff has arrived," Kayla replied.

They stepped into the en suite bathroom. Thankfully, it had a large soaking tub. "Let's get you settled in the tub."

"Um, Kayla."

"Yes."

"My water just broke." Tears streamed down Brenda's face.

"Oh, honey, it's going to be okay." Kayla prayed she was right and the momma and her baby would be okay.

She settled Brenda into the tub with a pillow behind her head. Then she dug around in the bathroom cabinet and located an extra-large towel that she handed to Brenda. "I need to go talk to Larry. He has to call an ambulance to take you to the hospital."

Brenda clutched Kayla's hand. "Don't leave me. I'm afraid if you go out of the room, he won't let you back in here. And I need you." A contraction hit, and she started her Lamaze breathing, squeezing Kayla's hand even tighter.

"You're doing great. I know the setting isn't ideal. But you can do this. You're a strong woman who is about to bring a beautiful baby girl into the world."

Larry rammed against the bedroom door and a splintering sound echo in the room. "Let me in."

"Stay away, Larry," Brenda yelled. "I'm having a baby and don't want you in here."

Kayla had to do something. Brenda's agitation wasn't good for her or the baby. If she didn't calm down, her blood pressure would spike and the situation would become even more dangerous.

She knew Heath was outside and was sure he was trying to devise a plan to get inside. Maybe she could take away Larry's gun, as she had out on the trail. But how? In the old Western TV shows, they usually had the men boil water when the women went into labor. Would that work? Could she use it as a weapon? Only one way to find out. She patted Brenda's hand then pulled her own hand free and stood in the bathroom doorway.

"Larry," she called, "if you want to be helpful, boil a pan of water."

"You think I got time to do that? The sheriff's outside threatening to shoot Joe unless he sees you."

Kayla glanced over at Brenda—her eyes rounded. Kayla shook her head and knelt beside the woman. "The sheriff would never do that. Believe me. Joe is not in danger."

"Even if he is," Brenda said softly, "he brought this on himself. My concern has to be for my baby girl, not her criminal daddy."

"Well, you need a peaceful environment to deliver that sweet baby." Kayla squeezed Brenda's shoulder. "I promise I'll be here with you, guiding you through this, but we need Larry to stop trying to break in the door."

She stepped into the bedroom. "Larry, this baby is ready to greet the world. I need that pan of hot water to sterilize the bathtub. I'll open the door when you come back with the water."

Kayla closed her eyes. *Please, Lord, let him believe me and don't let my plan backfire. Brenda and the baby need me.*

He walked away, his footsteps growing fainter as he left the hall. She breathed a sigh of temporary relief and went back to Brenda.

"I'm not really going to have the baby in the bathtub when there's a perfectly good bed in there, right?"

"No, ma'am. You will not have your baby in the bathtub. But you heard the gunshots. I don't know how much longer Heath—Sheriff Dalton—will wait before he charges in here. I can't risk you getting shot. So, I'm trying to think of a way for all of us to get out alive and safely transport you to the hospital… Unfortunately, I'll have to injure Larry to get his weapon away from him."

Brenda embraced Kayla. "Do whatever you have to do. Larry is out of control. He's not behaving like the brother I've spent my lifetime loving." A contraction hit and Brenda groaned in pain, squeezing Kayla so tightly she couldn't breathe.

Prying the woman's arms loose, she pulled back. "Breathe. Hee…hee…hoo… That's right. You've got this. You're a strong woman and you're going to raise a daughter that's going to be strong like her momma."

The contraction passed. Brenda rubbed her belly and smiled up at Kayla.

Kayla located a washcloth, dampened it in the sink and placed it on Brenda's forehead. "I promise, when we get out of here, I'll make sure the sheriff knows that you're not part of anything your brother or husband has done. And you didn't purposefully help abduct me. You're a victim, too."

"Thank you. I still can't believe how naïve I have been. I'm sorry for what my family has put you through. And for what you went through in the past with Lovelorn. You are the bravest woman I've ever met, and if I have to give birth in a cabin in the woods, I'm thankful you're here with me."

Brave. Kayla had never thought of herself as

brave, nor believed anyone else had either. She
would not let Brenda down. She would find a way
to save them both. Kayla heard a scraping noise
on the side of the cabin. Tugging her hand free
from Brenda, she put a finger to her lips. "Shh..."

Crossing into the bedroom, she went to the
window that overlooked the side yard and peered
out. A federal agent was crouched at the corner
of the cabin. The window was nailed shut, preventing Kayla from opening it. Larry had obviously thought of everything. The agent looked
up, startled.

"There's a woman in labor," she said in hushed
tones.

The agent shook his head. He couldn't understand her but she couldn't risk Larry hearing her.
It was obvious she had to communicate with the
officer without speaking. He had to know there
was a pregnant woman in labor so they didn't
storm inside the cabin and engage in a shoot-out.
Kayla checked all the drawers but couldn't find
paper or pencil. She went into the bathroom and
searched inside the cabinets. Grabbing a can of
shaving cream, she raced back to the window,
sprayed a liberal amount of cream on the glass
and spread it to create a smooth layer. Then she
carefully wrote *Woman in labor in this room!*
backward so the agent could read it. She'd known
all her years of sending messages back and forth
with her friend next door as a child when they'd

been shut indoors during winter snowstorms would pay off one day. The agent read her message and gave a nod. Then he mouthed, *Cabin surrounded stay in that room.*

"I have the water." Larry banged on the door.

Kayla grabbed a pillow off the bed and quickly wiped the window clean. Leaving the curtain slightly open, she prayed the agent would stay out of sight but also watch what transpired next. She crossed to the door.

"Thank you, Larry. Didn't you say Heath—I mean Sheriff Dalton—is here with Joe?"

"Yeah. I'm trying to decide what to do about that. I think you need to deliver that baby fast so he can see you."

"Larry, babies come in their own time. It could be thirty minutes or it could be three hours. Even longer. This isn't something I can control."

"Well, open the door. I'm tired of holding this pan of water."

Kayla glanced over her shoulder. She could see the agent as he looked through the window. *Please, Lord, don't let Larry notice him.* Huffing out a breath to still her nerves, she unlocked the door, pulled it open and stepped back.

Larry entered the room, a large steel pan in one hand and his rifle in the other. "Why isn't Brenda in the bed? Actually, now that I think about it, why is she giving birth in the bathtub?"

Honesty was the best policy, or so she'd always been told.

"When I heard gunshots earlier, I moved Brenda to the bathroom. It's an interior room, so I thought it would be safer. Now, she's in the bathtub," she replied loudly, hopeful the agent outside could hear.

Larry tilted his head and cocked an eyebrow. "That was smart thinking. I appreciate you helping my sister deliver my niece. Too bad I can't repay the favor and let you walk away when this is over."

Goose bumps popped out on Kayla's arms, and she struggled to resist the urge to run through the open door and race outside to Heath. Realistically, she knew she'd never make it. The killer would shoot her in the back. She pressed her lips together into a tight smile. "We all have to do what we have to do. Now, give me the pan."

"No." He held the large steel pan out of her reach. "I'll keep hold of this. Lead the way."

"But... Brenda is indisposed at the moment. She doesn't want—or need—her brother in there, seeing her like that."

"Listen to her," Brenda yelled from the bathroom. "I'm in the middle of a very traumatic experience at the moment. I don't need you in here seeing what God intended that I keep covered."

Larry stood still for a moment, staring at Kayla as if he couldn't decide what would be worse.

Hand a boiling pan of water over to her or defy his sister's wishes and see her disrobed. Finally, he turned the handle of the pan around for Kayla to grasp. She cautiously accepted it, careful not to burn herself on the metal.

He waved his weapon at her. "Take care of my sister."

"I will." She took a step toward the bathroom then, in one fluid movement, turned and tossed the boiling water into Larry's face. He screamed in pain, dropped the gun, clutched his face with both hands and fell to his knees.

Kayla grabbed the rifle and turned it on her tormentor. "We need an ambulance! Two of them!" she yelled at the top of her lungs. Fighting a wave of nausea, Kayla fought to stay upright on legs that no longer seemed to have the power to hold her up. *Lord, forgive me. I'm honor bound by duty to give aid to people in need. I'm not supposed to be the one causing them harm.*

# EIGHTEEN

"The nurse has disarmed the suspect!" Agent Knight yelled from the side of the cabin.

Heath raced toward the porch, charging up the steps a few feet ahead of Deputy Fisher and the FBI agents. He rammed against the door. It would not budge. Deputy Fisher joined him and, on the third attempt, the door popped open.

"Kayla! Where are you?" he yelled.

"Back here. In the bedroom!"

He charged down the hall and into the room where Kayla stood, holding Larry's rifle on him as he writhed in pain on the floor. His hair and shirt were wet and a kitchen pan lay a few feet away.

As agents surrounded Larry, Heath crossed to Kayla, shoved his pistol into his holster and carefully removed the rifle from her hands. "It's okay. You're safe now." Heath handed the rifle to Agent Knight, wrapped Kayla in his arms and held her tight, her body trembling.

"It's my job to give aide to people—to treat

their injuries. I'm not supposed to be the one inflicting harm." Her voice cracked as tears welled in her eyes.

He framed her face with his hands and brushed the hair out of her eyes. "You did what you had to do to survive. I'm so *proud* of you. You were so *brave*."

A guttural scream came from the bathroom. Kayla pushed away from Heath and ran into the small room.

He followed close behind. A pregnant woman, whom he assumed was Brenda, lay in the tub, obviously in active labor. He looked over his shoulder at Agent Knight, "Get your men and Larry out of here. We need to move Brenda onto the bed. If I'm not mistaken, this baby isn't going to wait for the ambulance to arrive."

The agent nodded and his men quickly grasped Larry by the upper arms and hauled him from the room.

Kayla met his eyes. "Have you ever delivered a baby before?"

"Once, when I was a rookie in Nashville, I assisted my partner when he delivered a baby in a vehicle that had broken down on the interstate. He did the actual delivering. So, you're in charge. I'll do what you say."

They helped Brenda to her feet and guided her to the bed, a large beach towel wrapped around her waist, keeping her modest. He eased Brenda onto the bed and rushed back to the bathroom to retrieve the pillows. When he returned, he tucked them behind the pregnant woman.

"Mrs. Granger, I'm Sheriff Dalton. If you don't mind, I'm going to assist Nurse Eldridge with your delivery."

"I don't mind you assisting. I do mind you calling me Mrs. Granger. It seems I don't even know anything about the man I married. So for right now, I'd prefer to just be Brenda. Okay? And drop the Nurse Eldridge formalities, too. Kayla and I have become fast friends." Brenda inhaled deeply and exhaled short bursts of breath. "It's amazing how quickly you can bond when you're thrown into a situation like this."

*Oh, how well Heath knew that statement to be true.* Heath couldn't help but look at Kayla. She was getting into position at the foot of the bed.

Heath turned his attention back to the woman who was about to give birth. "Brenda, if you don't mind, I will sit behind you on the bed to help support your back as you push this baby into the world."

"I'll take all the help I can get, Sheriff."

"Call me Heath. I believe we're about to become fast friends, too." He looked up and saw the biggest smile spread across Kayla's face. He didn't know what had put it there, but he was thankful to witness it.

Forty minutes later, a tiny baby girl with a

head full of curly brown hair lay swaddled in a pillowcase in her mama's arms, on top of a gurney about to be rolled out of the cabin by a paramedic and an EMT.

"Kayla, I can never thank you enough," Brenda said, tears streaming down her face. She turned to Heath. "I appreciate both of you so very much."

"You did all the work. We were just the coaches who cheered you on," Heath replied.

Kayla gave Brenda a hug. "Take care of that baby girl. I'll come by the hospital to check on you tomorrow."

The other woman nodded, then she looked at Heath. "Sheriff, I'll report to the station as soon as I'm released from the hospital."

"That's fine." He patted her shoulder. "Right now, I don't want you to worry about anything but bonding with that beautiful baby girl. We'll get a statement from you later."

"She wasn't part of this." Kayla shook her head, her eyes pleading with him. "Larry tricked her into going to the clinic. She didn't know what his intentions were."

"Don't worry. We'll sort it all out." Heath turned to the EMT. "You can take her now."

He and Kayla stepped out onto the small porch and watched as they loaded Brenda and her baby into the back of the ambulance.

Kayla rubbed her lower back. "This is not how

I thought the day was going to go after I walked into the clinic this morning."

"Same. When my dispatcher told me Larry and a pregnant woman had abducted you, I never expected to be involved in delivering the baby."

"Any news on Larry?"

"He's at the hospital being treated for some pretty nasty burns, but he'll be okay," Agent Knight replied as he came up behind them. "He'll probably have a scarred face once he's healed, but he'll live."

Kayla's eyes widened as she turned to Heath. "Will I face charges for hurting him?"

"It was self-defense, ma'am," Agent Knight answered before Heath could. "I witnessed the entire event."

"You were the agent under the window?"

"Yes, ma'am." He turned to Heath and held out his hand. "Sheriff, I'll be in touch soon about transferring Joe. I'm sure we'll see each other several times over the next few months." Agent Knight looked from Heath to Kayla. "I'll need a statement from you as well. You should expect a notice to appear in federal court when the case goes to trial."

"If this is a federal case, does that also mean Brenda's involvement in my abduction would fall under federal jurisdiction?" Kayla asked, concern evident in her voice.

"Yes, ma'am. After her release from the hospital, we'll bring her in for questioning. However, Larry stated multiple times on his ride to the hospital that his sister was innocent of all wrongdoing. He said she didn't know what his motives were. Do you agree with that?"

"Yes, sir. I saw the shock on her face when she realized she'd been deceived. It was heartbreaking. Then she tried to get Larry to turn himself in." She frowned. "Brenda had no clue her brother and husband were involved in drug trafficking."

"Fair enough. As far as I'm concerned, we'll treat Mrs. Granger as a witness and a victim, not as a suspect."

"Thank you," Kayla said.

Agent Knight gave a curt nod and walked away.

Kayla looked as if she was about to collapse from exhaustion. Heath put his arm around her and she rested her head on his shoulder. "Let me take you home."

"Going home sounds good," she replied. "But I want to go to the cabin, not Sawyer's. I need time alone to decompress."

He hated the idea of her being alone, but he also understood her need to have time to process all that had occurred.

As he guided her down the porch steps, a black SUV turned into the drive, going way too fast as it sped up the hill, gravel spitting out from under the tires. The SUV slammed to a stop behind his patrol vehicle. Bridget sat in the passenger seat with Sawyer behind the steering wheel. Uh-oh.

He jerked his head toward the vehicle. "Looks like you get to have the discussion about where you spend the night with your brother right now."

Bridget hopped out of the vehicle and rushed to meet Heath and Kayla at the foot of the stairs, just as the ambulance pulled out of the driveway, lights flashing.

"Who wants to fill me in on what happened here?" Sawyer demanded, jogging up to the group.

"Honey, give them a chance." Bridget chided her husband. Then she enveloped Kayla in a hug. "I'm so glad you're okay."

Heath dropped his arm, squared his shoulders and faced Sawyer. "I understand you're upset. When all of this happened, you were on a plane. There wasn't a way to notify you. And even if I could have, what would you have done besides worry?"

"He has a point there, dear." Bridget giggled.

The vein in Sawyer's neck twitched. After several long seconds, he held out his hand. Heath accepted the handshake and was quickly pulled into a one-armed hug. "Thank you for saving my sister."

Heath clapped Sawyer on the back and pulled away from the embrace. "I didn't save her. She saved herself. Then she delivered a baby. She is truly an amazing woman."

Sawyer narrowed his eyes as if he were trying to read Heath's mind, but he refused to look away. Heath was sure his friend was correctly assessing his feelings for his sister. And he didn't care. He wanted the world to know. Albeit, not before he told Kayla.

Sawyer gave a slight nod, turned to Kayla and pulled her into an embrace. "Thank the Lord, you're safe."

Kayla returned the hug, pulled back and smiled at her brother and sister-in-law. "I'm glad you're both home." She looked around. "Where's Vincent?"

"He's with my grandparents. We were at their house when we heard what happened. We'd stopped by to give them the latest update on Dad," Bridget replied.

"How is your father?" Heath asked.

"He's going to be fine."

"Now that the pleasantries are out of the way, who's going to fill me in on what happened and who was in the ambulance?" Sawyer queried.

"Joe Granger's wife and baby were in the ambul—"

"Can we save the play-by-play discussion for later?" Kayla asked. "I need food and a nap first."

"Sure. Let's get you home." Sawyer reached for Kayla's arm. She pulled back.

252 Smoky Mountain Escape

"I love you, big brother, and I'm so thankful for you. But I'm going back to the cabin," she declared in a no-nonsense tone and grasped Heath's arm. "And Heath will drive me."

"But—"

"*We* understand." Bridget cut off whatever Sawyer had been about to say. "Why don't both of you come to supper tonight?"

"Thanks, but could we make it Saturday night instead?" Kayla turned to Heath. "Would that be okay with you?"

"Sure, but I hate to intrude on a family dinner."

"It's no intrusion," the women said in unison.

Bridget and Kayla hugged. Then Bridget steered Sawyer to their vehicle while Kayla guided Heath to his. He smiled. He wasn't completely sure how Bridget and Kayla had done it, but they'd planned his Saturday night while stopping Sawyer from getting his way. And it was all fine by him. As long as he got to spend more time with the beautiful lady holding his arm, he couldn't ask for more in life.

Three days later, Kayla waved goodbye to Amos Cline as she pulled out of the parking lot of his auto shop. The kind mechanic had insisted on bringing her car to the rental company when she returned her rental. He'd planned to walk back to his shop—two miles away—but she'd convinced him to let her give him a ride. Everyone in Barton Creek amazed her with their kindness. Mrs. Frances had brought her a casserole the night before. And today, Dr. Lester was adamant she take off work two hours early to pick up her vehicle and have time to get ready for her dinner date—even though Kayla had repeatedly told her employer it wasn't a date, simply a family dinner. And all the patients she'd seen the past three days had expressed how they had prayed for her and were thankful she'd survived her ordeal. The entire community had embraced her.

And that was why she had made a major life-altering decision this afternoon that she was both excited and nervous to share with Heath and her family this evening.

Pulling into the driveway of the cabin, a feeling of being home washed over her. She sighed contentedly. When she moved out at the end of the month, she would miss the small, homey cabin. She was very thankful that Mrs. Frances understood her leaving two months earlier than planned. But sometimes something falls into place and you have to act on it quickly. And she was content that her decision was the right one.

She went inside, dropped her purse and keys on the table and immediately raced to the bedroom closet. What was she going to wear? She pulled out one outfit after the other until her eyes lit upon the lightweight floral cotton dress with cap sleeves she had purchased right before leaving the city. Paired with her wedge sandals and a pair of stud earrings, it would be perfect.

She showered, dried her hair, completed a light touch of makeup, got dressed and then waited for Heath to arrive. She felt giddy. Something she hadn't felt since the day Jonathan had proposed. If she was truly honest with herself, she hadn't felt as happy that day as she currently did.

The sound of a vehicle pulling up outside had her peeking through the blinds. It was Heath! He was early. She crossed to the front door and put her hand on the knob, her heart racing. While Kayla had spent the last few days evaluating her life—her accomplishments and what she wanted in the future—he had only called her once. She prayed it was simply because he'd been giving her time to process everything and decompress. If it was more than that—if he believed he had fulfilled his duty and they were nothing more than sheriff and citizen... She would accept it. Even if it wasn't what she wanted. No matter how this evening went, whether they could only be friends or they could pursue a more meaningful relationship, she was determined not to close her heart off to the world again. She was a survivor. But she wanted to do more than just survive. She wanted to thrive.

He rapped on the door. She exhaled a soft breath and opened it.

Heath stood in front of her, dressed in casual

slacks and a button-down shirt, a bouquet of sunflowers in his hand. "You are breathtaking." He leaned in and kissed her cheek. "These are for you."

"Thank you," she said, accepting the bouquet. "Let me find a vase for these before we leave."

He followed her inside. She opened several cabinets before selecting a tall glass to hold the flowers. She filled it with water and arranged them, then set them on the dining table.

"I'm sorry, I should have purchased a vase. I wasn't thinking."

"Nope. I think this is perfect."

Heath caught her by the shoulders and turned her to face him, searching her face. "You look rested and…happy."

She offered a closed-lipped smile and nodded.

He captured her hand and led her to the sofa. "Could we talk a few minutes before heading to Sawyer's?"

"Sure." She settled onto the couch and turned to face him.

He looked down at their hands, his thumb caressing the back of hers. "How are you, really?"

"I am…" How could she describe the transformation that had taken place in her heart since Wednesday? "I'm wonderful. It's difficult to put into words but, emotionally, I feel like the clock has rewound four years. Only, I'm wiser than I had been at twenty-two."

She met his eyes. "The baggage from the trauma that Jonathan and Larry have put me through will always be with me, but somehow I have managed to tuck it away in a smaller corner of my mind to where it's not all-consuming."

"That makes my very happy. You will not believe how many times I picked up the phone to call you, only to put it down because I wanted to respect your wishes of time alone to get into the groove of daily life and to process everything."

"It might surprise you to know I almost called you numerous times, too. Only, I knew you would be busy dealing with everything related to this case."

They sat in silence for a few minutes, just holding hands.

"I'm—"

"May—"

They laughed.

"You first," Heath said.

"I visited Brenda yesterday before they released her from the hospital. She and the baby were both doing well. I was just wondering if she had had her interview with you and Agent Knight yet. I don't want her to face repercussions for her brother and her husband's actions. She truly is innocent."

"We interviewed her this morning. Agent Knight's investigation over the past few days has uncovered a lot of illegal activities that tie back to some really dangerous people. He's going over the evidence—what part he can—with Brenda. He suspects, even though she was not a participant in the illegal activities, that she may unknowingly have information that could be dangerous for her. So, she'll be in protective custody until the hearings are over."

"I won't be able to visit her and the baby again?"

"I'm afraid not. At least for a while." He looked down at their hands again. "Most likely, you will have moved on to your next assignment before she's out of protective custody."

"About that… I was going to wait and tell you when I told Sawyer and Bridget but…"

Heath jerked his head upward, sadness evident in his eyes. "That's why you look so happy. You're moving to your next assignment early, escaping the horrible memories in Barton Creek."

"No. The opposite. The nurse I am filling in for has decided not to come back. She's going to stay home with her new infant. Dr. Lester offered me the job full-time. I accepted it and rented Jenna Quinn's house. It's been vacant since she married Sean last year. She offered me a deal I couldn't turn down."

Heath whooped and pulled her into an embrace. "I was so afraid you were leaving."

She pulled back. "I'm glad you're happy that I'm staying."

"Happy? I'm ecstatic! I've been considering becoming a transient myself, just so I could follow you from place to place."

Kayla laughed. "Why would you do that?"

"How else could we date?"

She sobered. "You want to date me?"

"Well, yes. But I hadn't really planned to have that discussion tonight. I wanted to consider my career options and give you time to realize that you like me as much as I like you." He smiled, dropped her hand and shoved his hand through his hair. "That sounded conceited, didn't it? I didn't mean it that way. But we are good together. Look how we survived in the woods. I trust you to always have my back. And I enjoy your company and—"

She leaned in and kissed him, silencing whatever he'd been about to say. He wrapped his arms around her and drew her close. Several long seconds later, she pulled back and smiled at him. "Heath Dalton, I am head-over-heels for you. It's the main reason I decided to stay in Barton Creek. I had hoped if I did, you might realize how much you like me."

A smile spilt his face. "I don't deserve a woman as amazing as you. And, just so you know, I'm looking into other career options. I thought I might see if Parker would let me be a partner in his camping gear business. Or maybe—"

"Why?" She frowned. "I thought you loved being the sheriff."

"I do, but I love you more."

"Is there a reason you can't love both?"

He pulled her hand to his lips and kissed the back of it. "I would rather walk away from law enforcement than risk ever putting you in danger again."

"And I would rather have a happy, fulfilled hus—boyfriend—than to have one who sacrificed his career for me when it wasn't in his best interest. Besides, I refuse to live my life in fear any longer."

"You almost said 'husband.'" He grinned and her face warmed. "I love you, Kayla Eldridge."

"And I love you, Heath Dalton."

He claimed her lips once more and her heart swelled with joy.

*Thank you, Lord, for seeing me through the valley of darkness and guiding me to this new mountaintop, blessing me beyond measure.*

# EPILOGUE

*One year later*

Crossing to the window, Kayla pulled back the curtain. Fat raindrops fell from the sky, the thirsty ground soaking up the water like a sponge. "Looks like the draught is over," she laughed and turned to her mom and bridesmaids, Bridget and Jenna.

"How can you look so happy?" Mom asked, coming to stand beside her. "You refused to make a backup plan. What are we going to do now?"

"I *am* happy. It's my wedding day." She pulled her mom into a hug. "Besides, Heath and I met during a rainstorm. It's only fitting that we get married during one, too."

"But your dress and your hair—"

"Will be beautiful, no matter what. But only if she sits back down and lets me put on the finishing touches." Bridget stood in the doorway of her en suite bathroom, one hand on her hip and the other pointing to the stool in front of the vanity mirror.

Kayla smiled, kissed her mom's cheek and followed her sister-in-law's command. "I can't thank you and Sawyer enough for letting us have the ceremony here."

"No thanks necessary. We're family. And we're both so happy for you and Heath. You deserve all the happiness in the world."

Twenty minutes later, the rain was still falling but her mood had only brightened. Bridget had arranged her hair in a half-up, half-down style with the sides pulled back off her face and captured in a rhinestone clip, while the back hung in curly waves.

Bridget zipped the back of Kayla's flowy, blush-colored, A-line, full-length wedding dress. "There."

Kayla twirled around.

"Oh, Kayla. You're stunning," Jenna affirmed.

"My baby." Mom dabbed her eyes with the lace-edged handkerchief Kayla had given her for the occasion.

"Your baby is about to be a married lady."

"I know. I'm so happy for you. And I pray you and Heath are as happy as your dad and I were."

Kayla smiled. A marriage like her parents had had was something she'd always dreamed of having. They'd only had eighteen years together, but

Kayla had felt honored to witness fifteen of those years, seeing how a man should treat a woman. A few months before he passed, her dad had told her he'd been an immature boy the first time he'd married and he had many regrets about the way he'd handled everything. When he'd fallen in love with her mom, he'd been determined to be the man she deserved.

She hated that Sawyer had grown up without knowing Dad the way she had, but she'd seen many of their father's traits in her brother and was thankful he'd welcomed her mom into his life this past year. He'd never think of her as his stepmom. But because of their shared love for Kayla, they had found a way to become a family. And that made her heart happy.

She took a deep breath and slowly released it. "Okay, let's go. I'm ready to see my groom."

"But it's still raining." Mom stated the obvious.

"I know—"

There was a knock on the bedroom door. Bridget crossed and opened it. Sawyer entered.

"I wanted to—" He spotted Kayla and gasped. "You. Look. Beautiful."

Tears gathered in her eyes. She had missed out on having a big brother as a child, but she couldn't imagine her life without him now. Her dad wasn't here, but every time she looked at Sawyer, she saw him. "Don't make me cry."

Someone pushed a tissue into her hand, and she dabbed her eyes as he gathered her into a big hug.

"Don't wrinkle my dress." She playfully swatted his arm.

"Oh. I'm sorry." He stepped back sheepishly.

"What did you come to tell us?" Bridget asked.

Kayla inhaled sharply. "Did Heath change his mind? Am I getting stood up?"

"Kayla. You know better," Jenna chided, walking over and putting her arm around Kayla. "That man loves you. Now, let's hear what Sawyer has to say."

"According to the radar, there should be a break in the rain in an hour. The preacher was wondering if you wanted to delay—"

"No. Not a chance." She shook her head vehemently.

"But—"

"Did you ask Heath?" Kayla questioned.

"Yes."

"What did he say?"

A smile split Sawyer's face. "Not a chance."

Her heart swelled. "Well, there you go."

"Okay, then. Let's get you two hitched." He opened the door wide. Standing in the hall were the groomsmen, each with an oversized umbrella in his hand.

Deputy Fisher offered his elbow to Kayla's mom. "Ma'am. May I escort you?"

She kissed Kayla's cheek. "I love you." Then she accepted the arm and walked out of the room. Jenna and Sean followed them, with Bridget and Parker close behind.

Sawyer picked her bouquet of yellow roses up off the dresser and handed it to her. "I never imagined I'd be giving away a bride before I ever had a daughter."

"It's always good to have a practice run." She accepted the flowers and slipped her hand through the crook of his elbow. "Your little girl will be blessed to have you for a dad."

"Bridget told you." He frowned. "We were going to wait until you returned from your honeymoon."

"She let it slip last night at the rehearsal dinner when I found her in the ladies' room... the appetizers had made her nauseous." Kayla hugged Sawyer. "I'm so happy for you both and can't wait to see Vincent as a big brother."

He placed his hand over hers that rested on his arm. "Let's get going or your groom may start to wonder if you're standing him up."

They made their way through the house to the French doors in the family room that lead out into the backyard. Looking through the glass, she could see that the guests had been seated at the tables in the large, white reception tent, the side flaps pulled back and fastened to allow a clear view of the ceremony. Her mother was in a place of honor closest to the ceremony area where the preacher stood in front of the wooden arbor, adorned with white lights. A Bible in one hand and an umbrella in the other. Heath stood beside him with an extra-large umbrella. And the matron of honor and best man—Bridget and Parker—stood on each side of him, umbrellas clutched in their hands and big smiles on their faces.

*We are truly blessed to have people who love us enough to stand beside us on rainy days.*

"It's time," Sawyer said.

She nodded. They walked out onto the small covered patio and made their way across the lawn. Heath met them halfway. He took her hand, and she stepped under the shelter of his umbrella. Every cell in her body quaked with excitement. This man was the love of her life, her protector and best friend.

"You are so beautiful," Heath whispered. "I love you."

"I love you, too."

"I'm sorry it's raining."

"I'm not." She smiled. "Our love story began on a rainy day, so it's only fitting that our marriage does, too."

He squeezed her hand. "I promise to always

be your safe place and your shelter for all the days—sunny or rainy—for the rest of our lives."

Tears of joy leaked out of her eyes. "Let's do this."

She rested her hand on the crook of his arm, a huge smile on her face as they took the first step to their happily-ever-after.

\* \* \* \* \*

*If you liked this story from Rhonda Starnes,*
*check out her previous*
*Love Inspired Suspense books:*

Rocky Mountain Revenge
Perilous Wilderness Escape
Tracked Through the Mountain
Abducted at Christmas
Uncovering Colorado Secrets
Cold Case Mountain Murder

*Available now from Love Inspired Suspense!*
*Find more great reads at*
*www.LoveInspired.com.*

Dear Reader,

When I first *met* Kayla, while writing *Rocky Mountain Revenge*, I knew she had to have a story of her own. It was just a matter of waiting for the right hero to come along.

Life is a series of mountains and valleys. When we're traveling in the valley, we must support each other and rely on God to see us through it. And when we're on the mountaintop, we must remember to be grateful for all of life's blessings and appreciate those who helped lift us up when we were down.

Heath and Kayla were both traveling in the valley when they met, but their love for God and each other soon had them soaring to the mountaintop.

I would love to hear from you. Please connect with me at www.rhondastarnes.com and follow me on Facebook @authorrhondastarnes.

All my best,
*Rhonda Starnes*